ETERNAL QUEST

PRATIK PATNAIK

Made with ♥ on the Notion Press Platform
www.notionpress.com

To Baba and Mama, for their unwavering support, my sister Pratikhya, for igniting the love towards stories, my wife Silpa, for her love and belief in me, and my son Viaansh, who inspires me every day.

And to all my well wishers and friends

—this book is for you

Contents

Acknowledgements

From childhood, I have been fascinated by mythological stories and characters. They have fueled my curiosity and imagination, making me wonder "What if?"—creating endless possibilities where legends could be reimagined, expanded, or seen from a different lens. These stories have stayed with me, whispering new ideas and sparking the desire to tell my own.

Though I am an engineer by profession, art and literature have always been more than just hobbies; they have been a passion, a creative refuge where I find fulfillment. This book is my humble attempt to bring to life a story that I would love to hear—one that stretches the boundaries of imagination and ventures into the unexplored realms of mythology.

I do not claim to be an expert in mythological tales, nor do I think I ever will be. Learning, reading, and listening to these stories will always be a journey—one that I will continue to embrace with an open heart and an eager mind. This novel is a product of that journey, born from my imagination and nurtured with dedication, countless hours of effort, and an unwavering love for storytelling.

To all the writers who have inspired me—thank you. Your words, your worlds, and your unwavering passion for storytelling have kept me going, urging me to complete this humble effort.

This is my first creation that I am sharing with the world, and I hope it is just the beginning of many more to come.

Prologue

In ancient times, when gods and demons were locked in an eternal struggle for supremacy, the cosmic ocean of milk, Kshira Sagara, lay dormant, holding within its depths the secret of immortality. This elixir, Amrita, was the prize Devas (gods) and Asuras (demons) sought. In their ceaseless quest, an uneasy truce was forged between the two factions to churn the ocean together, for neither could achieve this feat alone.

The setting was grand and cosmic, with Mount Mandara towering as the churning rod, resting on the back of the giant tortoise avatar of Lord Vishnu, Kurma, who was a pivot. The great serpent Vasuki was chosen as the churning rope. The Devas, led by Indra, took the tail, wary of the serpent's venomous head, which the Asuras, led by the mighty Bali, accepted with hubris and disdain. The sky was a riot of colors, an aurora of divine light and chaotic energy, as the Devas and Asuras took their positions. The churning began with a synchronized heave, causing the ocean to roil and froth. As they pulled back and forth, the mighty Vasuki coiled around Mount Mandara, the mountain groaned, and the waves surged, crashing against the celestial shore with a thunderous roar.

Initially, the churning brought forth a series of wonders and horrors from the ocean's depths. Dark, noxious fumes rose, spreading poison and threatening to shroud the world in a deadly haze. The Devas and Asuras paused in horror, but Lord Shiva, ever the protector, intervened. He drank the poison, which turned his throat blue, earning him the name Neelkanth. His act of sacrifice averted disaster, allowing the churning to continue.

With renewed vigor, the Devas and Asuras resumed their task. From the depths emerged the divine cow, Kamadhenu, the source of all desires, claimed by the sages for their sacrifices to use the milk produced by the cow to prepare ghee for the yagnas. Next came the celestial tree, Parijat, with flowers of unmatched fragrance and beauty, and the gem, Kaustubha, which Lord Vishnu adorned. Each emergence was a marvel, adding to the cosmic splendor. Then appeared the goddess Lakshmi, radiant and resplendent, who chose Lord Vishnu as her consort, bestowing upon him the fortune and prosperity of the universe. The Asuras and Devas watched in awe and envy, but the ultimate prize, the Amrita, was yet to surface.

Finally, the ocean trembled and heaved as Dhanvantari, the divine physician, rose with the pot "Kalash" of Amrita. The sight of the coveted elixir incited greed and lust among the Asuras. Both factions lunged forward, attempting to seize the pot forcefully, disrupting the fragile alliance. A fierce struggle ensued, with the Devas and Asuras clashing, each side desperate to claim immortality.

Amidst the turmoil, Lord Vishnu emerged in the mesmerizing form of Mohini. Her beauty was otherworldly, her charm irresistible. Both Devas and Asuras were mesmerized, their conflict momentarily forgotten. Mohini offered to distribute the Amrita, and the enchanted Asuras eagerly agreed, unaware of the deception. With graceful movements, Mohini began distributing the Amrita to the Devas first. The Asuras, captivated by her beauty, watched in dazed acquiescence. Svarbhanu, an Asura, saw through the trickery and disguised himself as a Deva, slipping into the line. As the Amrita touched his lips, Surya (The Sun) and Chandra (The Moon) alerted Mohini, who swiftly decapitated him. Rahu, his head, having tasted the elixir, became immortal, forever chasing the Sun and Moon in vengeance, causing eclipses.

After the war and the distribution of Amrit to the Devas, they became stronger and mightier than ever before. However, during the chaos and conflict between the Devas and Asuras, a few drops of the elixir spilled from the Amrit Kalash and fell onto the surface of the Earth. Additionally, some drops from the elixir en route to Rahu's body also fell to the Earth after his beheading. The Asuras, eager to gain the boon of immortality, sought these scattered drops.

Alarmed by this pursuit, the Devas pleaded with Lord Vishnu to intervene.

After hearing the Devas' plea, Lord Vishnu rested in a calm posture, his serene smile radiating assurance. With infinite grace, he exuded tranquility, embodying divine confidence. His presence alone soothed the worried Devas as they sensed his readiness to protect and restore balance.

CHAPTER ONE

THE SEEKERS

October 2017

There lay a warehouse in the heart of Varanasi, amidst the labyrinthine streets echoing with the chants of ancient prayers and the Ghats bustling with spiritual fervor. This inconspicuous building, tucked away behind a row of vibrant market stalls, was a treasure trove of history. Here, Arvind Mishra, the fourth-generation heir to a legacy of book collectors, had his sanctuary. In his late forties, Arvind carried an aura that blended seamlessly with the mystique of his surroundings. His charming demeanor and sharp intellect had earned him a reputation that preceded him. He sat in his cluttered yet meticulously organized office, a space overflowing with an eclectic mix of books, manuscripts, and artifacts that whispered stories from centuries past.

The wooden desk before him creaked under the weight of ancient texts and fragile manuscripts. However, Arvind's attention was riveted on a particular artifact—a piece of Brahmi script inscribed on a weathered palm leaf. His dark eyes, intense and focused, trace the elegant curves and lines of the ancient characters. The dim light of the single lamp on his desk cast a warm glow, creating a cocoon of concentration around him, isolating him from the chaotic vibrancy outside. From Sanskrit scrolls to Persian poetry, each item had a designated place, reflecting Arvind's painstaking dedication to preserving his heritage. The office room had meticulously arranged shelves that exuded the rich scent of aged paper and leather, mingled with the faint hint of incense, a constant reminder of the city's spiritual essence.

Arvind's journey to this moment had been one of passion and perseverance. He often traversed great distances, from the remote villages of Rajasthan to the dense forests of Kerala, in search of forgotten treasures. His charm and people skills were his greatest assets. With a disarming smile and an encyclopedic knowledge of history, he persuaded reluctant sellers to see the value of their forgotten heirlooms by weaving eloquent tales. His charisma and eloquence left them in awe, often parting with their treasures with a sense of honor rather than loss.

As Arvind methodically deciphered an ancient script, his mind danced through possibilities. This artifact could be a key to unlocking a forgotten chapter of history. His fingers lightly brushed over the delicate surface of a scroll made out of cotton, and he began to jot down notes in his leather-bound journal, his handwriting was a blend of fluidity and precision. Every discovery and every piece of information was another stitch in the intricate tapestry of human history he was so passionately dedicated to preserving.

For over a week, Arvind Mishra had been engrossed in deciphering the same seven lines of a scroll. It was very much him to be so fixated on ancient and antique items, but something about this fragment had ensnared his curiosity. Each day, he poured over the delicate strokes, his mind was tirelessly working to unlock its secrets. However, he felt different. As he traced the final character, a sudden realization dawned upon him. His heart raced; it was a eureka moment. He had been working on this project for decades and finally, he could reach some significant milestone that could show the path ahead.

His eyes widened with excitement as he comprehended the hidden meaning within the lines. He had worked tirelessly in the last few years on this. Hastily, he grabbed his phone, his fingers trembling with anticipation. Scrolling through his contacts, he found the number he sought and pressed call. The phone rang only once before a familiar voice answered.

"Professor Rao," Arvind began, barely able to contain his excitement,

"I think I've found something extraordinary. I think all our theories and stories about the ultimate quest could be true. In the last few days, I have checked all our data and findings, which are all pointing to the same thing. I have put together the next course of action"

There was a moment of stunned silence on the other end before the professor responded, his voice tinged with equal parts amazement and curiosity.
"Arvind, this could be groundbreaking. We need to discuss this immediately with the group."

"Give me a couple of hours to verify again."

"Ok."

Every evening, after a day spent in study and occasional teaching, Professor Rao had a routine of unwinding in front of the television, catching up on the latest news. He had settled into his favorite armchair, a humble but comfortable piece of furniture that had supported him through many such quiet evenings. The news channels flickered with the day's events, ranging from politics to local happenings and international affairs. As a scholar, he appreciated staying informed about the world, seeing it as a way to connect his academic interests with contemporary issues.

It was during this serene evening that Professor Rao received a phone call to his mobile. The ringtone, a classical melody, cut through the ambient noise of the television. Rao reached for the phone, expecting it. The conversation that followed was brief but exhilarating. As he hung up, a palpable excitement radiated from him, transforming his usually calm demeanor.

"Thank you, Arvind, I will intimate the group and prepare to meet on the 9th Oct evening."

"I have got a plan to verify the artifacts, please ask Gautam and Raghavan to bring with them their pieces, I will speak with Amara" Arvind replied.

"Also bring the letter and other information that you have from your grandfather." He added.

"Let us not discuss here much, we never know who is spying on us. Maintain the secrecy that we have been maintaining for years now. Everyone knows what to bring." Rao responded in a voice of authority.

"What about ....." As Arvind was going to complete his question, Rao interrupted him.

"See you soon." And he disconnected the call.

Professor Ramkumar Rao, a distinguished scholar with an MA in Hindu Studies and a PhD in Theology, resided in the serene and historic town of Berhampur, Odisha. His modest 3BHK flat, though simple, was a treasure trove of knowledge, filled with ancient texts, scriptures, and research papers orderly arranged on sturdy wooden shelves. The scent of old books circulated with the aroma of incense, creating an atmosphere of calm and contemplation. Rao was well-known in academic circles for his profound understanding of Hindu scriptures and mythology. He had expertise in the Vedas, Upanishads, Mahabharata, Ramayana, and countless other texts that form the bedrock of Hindu philosophy and spirituality. His intellectual curiosity extended beyond theology; he had a keen interest in archaeology and followed developments in the field with great enthusiasm. The intersection of historical findings with ancient scriptures was a subject that fascinated him deeply, which often led to rich discussions with his peers and students.

With hands folded and closed eyes, he offered a brief prayer. As the evening progressed, Professor Rao's thoughts were consumed by this new development. The news channels continued their broadcast, but in his mind, a new narrative was unfolding — one where the ancient past met the present, promising a future rich with understanding and enlightenment.

It was early October, and Indore awakened to a serene, crisp morning. The air was cool, carrying the faint scent of blooming flowers and dewy grass. Streets were bathed in the soft, golden glow of the rising sun, casting long shadows. Birds chirped melodiously, heralding the dawn. Vendors had set up their stalls, their vibrant produce was adding splashes of color to the scene. The hustle of daily life gradually picked up as people, wrapped in light shawls, began their day with steaming cups of chai. The city, in its tranquil beauty, reflected a harmonious blend of nature and early morning activity.

In his late forties, Dr. Rakesh Varma had built a reputable career in medicine, practicing in some of the most renowned hospitals in Indore and Ujjain. His medical expertise, coupled with his unwavering punctuality and warm rapport with patients and staff, had solidified his standing in the community as a dependable and highly skilled doctor.

Dr. Varma stood before the mirror in his elegantly furnished bedroom, meticulously adjusting his tie. The first rays of the morning sun filtered through the curtains, casting a warm glow on the room. It was a routine he had perfected over the years: a crisp white shirt, a neatly tied tie, and a calm, composed demeanor ready to face another day at the hospital.

Just as he was about to pick up his stethoscope, his phone, kept on the nightstand, buzzed. An unknown number flashed on the screen. With a furrowed brow, he picked up the call.

"Dr. Rakesh Varma speaking," he answered in his usual calm tone.

There was a brief pause before a voice, low and urgent, began to speak on the other end. Dr. Varma listened intently, his expression betraying no emotion. As the caller continued, he nodded occasionally, a sign of his attentive listening. The conversation was brief but laden with significance.

"I understand. I'll make the necessary arrangements," he replied before ending the call.

Without missing a beat, Dr. Varma dialed the hospital's number. The receptionist picked up after the first ring.

"Good morning, Dr. Varma," she greeted.

"Good morning. I need you to cancel all my appointments for the next one week" he said, his voice was steady and authoritative. "An emergency has come up that requires my immediate attention."

"Of course, Dr. Varma. I'll inform the patients and reschedule their appointments," the receptionist replied, accustomed to his professionalism.

"Thank you," he said, ending the call.

With the formalities taken care of, Dr. Varma turned and made his way to the kitchen. The scent of freshly brewed coffee and sizzling spices filled the air, a familiar comfort in his household. His wife, Anjali, stood at the stove, preparing breakfast. She glanced up as he entered, her face lighting up with a warm smile.

"Rakesh, breakfast is almost ready," she said, her eyes sparkling with love and warmth.

He walked over and gently placed a hand on her shoulder. "Anjali, I received a call this morning. The group is going to meet up, it seems we have got something significant."

Her eyes widened slightly, a mix of concern and curiosity flashing across her face. "Is everything okay?"

He nodded, his expression softening as he looked into her eyes. "Yes, it's something important. But it's also something that brings us hope and happiness."

They both shared a look of mutual trust and understanding. They had shared countless dreams and secrets over the years, and this was one more moment that bound them together.

Anjali's eyes shimmered with a mixture of hope and joy. "You think it could be...?"

Dr. Varma's lips curved into a small, reassuring smile. "Yes, I believe it could be a significant step forward."

She reached up and touched his cheek, her hand warm and reassuring. "Then go, Rakesh. Do what you need to do. I'll take care of everything here."

He leaned in and kissed her forehead gently. "Thank you, Anjali. Your support means everything to me."

As he walked away, ready to embark on yet another journey into the unknown, Dr. Rakesh Varma felt a renewed sense of purpose. The call had reignited a spark within him, a reminder of why he pursued the path he did, despite its moral complexities. As he stepped out of the house, the look of hope and happiness he had shared with his wife lingered in his mind, propelling him forward into the day ahead.

In Thiruvananthapuram, on the southern coast of India, lived an enigmatic owner of one of the most sought-after dress boutiques in the town, Amara Devika, a woman of striking beauty and unparalleled charm. In her mid-forties, she possessed an allure that transcended age, her every movement imbued with a grace that captivated all who crossed her path. Her boutique was located in a quaint corner of the bustling city and was a testament to her impeccable taste and keen eye for fashion. Silk saris of every hue, intricately embroidered lehengas, and elegant Western attire lined the walls, each piece was handpicked by Amara herself. Her clientele, a mix of the city's elite and fashion-conscious youth, were drawn not only by the exquisite garments but also by the magnetic presence of Amara Devika. Amara's beauty was more than skin deep; it was a carefully cultivated façade, a mask that had hidden her true nature. Her dark, kohl-rimmed eyes, often seen as pools of mystery and seduction, were windows to a soul steeped in secrets. During the day, she moved through her boutique with an air of confidence and warmth, engaging customers with her honeyed voice and bewitching smile. Men and women alike found themselves irresistibly drawn to her, often spending more than they had intended, enchanted by her persuasive charm.

Amara's house settled in a quiet neighborhood of Thiruvananthapuram, exuded an old-world charm that belied its occupant's enigmatic nature. The two-story structure painted a serene shade of white, stood gracefully amidst a lush garden filled with flowering plants and towering coconut trees. A cobblestone path led to the intricately carved wooden door, which opened into a spacious living room adorned with antique furniture and soft, muted colors. Her bedroom, located on the second floor, was a sanctuary of elegance and mystery. The room was spacious, with high ceilings and large windows draped with heavy, burgundy curtains that allowed only slivers of the bright Kerala sun to filter through. The walls were painted a deep, rich blue, giving the space an air of quiet sophistication. An ornate chandelier hung from the ceiling, casting a warm, golden glow over the room.

In one corner of the bedroom stood a full-length mirror framed in dark mahogany, its surface reflected the luxurious interior. In front of this mirror, Amara stood, a vision of timeless beauty. Her long, dark hair cascaded over her shoulders and glinted in the soft light as she carefully combed through it. The dark kohl around her eyes enhanced their depth, adding to the aura of mystery that surrounded her. Across the room, a wooden almirah occupied another corner. Its doors were carved with intricate floral patterns, and it held many of Amara's secrets within its depths. The almirah was both a treasure chest and a guardian of her hidden world.

As Amara ran the comb through her hair, she suddenly heard a faint buzz emanating from the almirah. The sound was soft but persistent, cutting through the stillness of the room. It was like a phone kept in vibration mode. Her heart skipped a beat, and she quickly put down the comb, her eyes narrowed in suspicion and curiosity. She ran across the room with a sense of urgency, her bare feet barely made a sound on the polished wooden floor. Reaching the almirah, Amara fumbled with the key, her hands trembled slightly. She unlocked the heavy doors and swung them open revealing a collection of neatly arranged items – jewelry, silk sarees, and an assortment of small, mysterious boxes. But by the time she peered inside, the buzzing had stopped. The silence that followed was almost deafening, amplifying her frustration and curiosity as she looked at the screen of the mobile phone. She stood there for another few minutes holding the phone in hand, expecting a call but it was all in vain.

She kept the phone inside the almirah, tucked it beneath her red Kanchipuram silk saree, and then locked the doors with a resolute click. With a practiced motion, she placed the key on top of the almirah, a curious ritual shared by many women.

This practice of locking the almirah only to leave the key in plain sight paradoxically undermined the very notion of security it was meant to uphold.

She returned to the mirror to get ready and completed her daily beauty rituals with meticulous care. She picked up her black handbag and checked the contents to ensure she hadn't forgotten anything before leaving for her boutique. Satisfied, she grabbed her lunchbox, a double-stack tin container wrapped in thin plastic. That morning, she had prepared Puttu and black channa curry, a meal she looked forward to enjoying for lunch.

Just as she was getting out of her bedroom, she heard the buzz again. This time she was swift to react. She quickly unlocked her almirah and grabbed the phone, without checking who the caller was, she took the call and placed it in her left ear. She knew who the caller was. The call didn't go for more than thirty seconds and she just listened to the caller with a few intermittent nods of acknowledgment. Once the call was over, she quickly grabbed another mobile from her black handbag and called someone.

"Vidhya, I will not be coming to the boutique for the next few days. Can you take the keys from me and manage the shop till I return?"

She paused for a response from the other side.

"Thank you. I am at home now, please come to collect it."

Her tone was both excited and nervous. She had a hint of sweat on her forehead, which she dabbed with her saree, which was very unlike her character.

She began exploring options on a travel app, planning a trip to some destination. After a few minutes, she placed the second phone back into her handbag. Switching off her other phone, she returned it to the almirah, pulling out a small stack of sarees as she did so. From beneath her bed, she retrieved a small rectangular lavender suitcase and began packing her belongings for the trip.

At the same time in Rameswaram, a small island town surrounded by the sea, a gentle, golden light, cast long shadows across the narrow streets and illuminated the shores where waves whispered ancient secrets. At the edge of this sacred town, where the sea embraced the land, stood a modest shop, its wooden sign swinging softly in the breeze: "Shanti's Treasures." Inside, among the array of seashells, corals, and antiques, a man moved with deliberate grace, his hands worn but steady, his eyes reflecting a soul deepened by trials.

Raghavan, the shop's owner, had once been a revered priest, his life devoted entirely to the service of God. For over two decades, he had been the heart of the temple, his days filled with prayers, rituals, and the comforting guidance he offered to the devotees. But fate, with its cruel twist, had torn him from his sanctified world. Accused of stealing the very ornaments he had sworn to protect, Raghavan had spent three harrowing years in jail, the stain of the false accusation forever marking his spirit.

Now in his late forties, Raghavan began each day in solitude. As dawn broke over Rameswaram, he walked to the shore, the rhythmic sound of the waves provided a serene backdrop to his thoughts. This morning was no different. He approached his shop, the salty air filling his lungs, and paused at the threshold, a silent prayer formed on his lips. His prayer was not one of words but of heartfelt surrender, a dialogue with the divine that transcended his circumstances. He lit a small lamp, its flame flickered gently and placed it before a modest idol of Lord Shiva, the deity he still served in his heart.

Raghavan then set about opening his shop. He unlatched the shutters, allowing the warm sunlight to stream in, illuminating the treasures he had painstakingly collected. Each item in his shop had a story, a fragment of the sea's timeless narrative. Seashells of various shapes and colors were arranged meticulously, each one polished to a soft sheen. Antique artifacts, some of which had been passed down through generations, were displayed with reverence. His hands, once skilled in performing intricate temple rituals, now gently handled these relics of nature and history.

With a cloth in hand, Raghavan carefully dusted the shelves, each stroke an act of penance and redemption. His movements were deliberate, almost meditative, as if each artifact he cleaned was a prayer, each polished shell a whispered plea for peace. The morning sun rose higher, casting a warm glow inside the shop, and the first visitors began to trickle in. Tourists drawn by the allure of the sea, and locals seeking a piece of their heritage, all were greeted with a soft smile and kind eyes.

"How much is this for?" Asked the tourist.

Snuggled among the treasures in Raghavan's shop was a unique shell, no more than a couple of inches in size. Its surface shimmered with a deep, oceanic blue, evoking the mystery of the sea. Intricately etched into the shell were serpentine designs, winding and intertwining with an almost hypnotic grace. The serpents' scales caught the light, creating a mesmerizing dance of shadows and highlights. This shell, with its rare color and detailed engravings, seemed to whisper ancient tales of the ocean's depths, captivating all who beheld it.

"Sorry Madam, that is not for sale."

Raghavan swiftly approached the visitor, his hand reached for the shell kept on the shelf. With a practiced motion, he retrieved it and carefully slipped it into his pocket. The evening prior, after closing the shop and enduring a power outage, he had taken the shell out of his small cash box to polish it. In the ensuing darkness, he had forgotten to return it to its place before closing up for the night.

"Ok, No problem."

The visitor responded with a surprised look.

"Till what time are you open today? I am in a hurry now, but wanted to buy some items before I leave tomorrow morning"

"I am closing today at noon. The shop will remain closed for the next few days. I am traveling out of town"

The sun began its ascent over the bustling city of Surat, casting a golden hue across the skyline and illuminating the opulent terrace of one of the city's most luxurious homes. Here, perched like a king surveying his realm, stood Gautam Mehta, a titan of the gems and gold industry. At sixty-six, Gautam embodied the very essence of affluence and success. His expansive frame, a testament to his unapologetic indulgence in the finer things of life, was adorned with an array of glittering gold chains and rings that sparkled in the morning light. The terrace itself was a testament to his wealth and taste. Sprawling and exquisitely designed, it offered a panoramic view of Surat's sprawling urban landscape, the glittering Tapi River, and the distant emerald fields. Lush potted plants and intricate marble flooring added to the elegance, while ornate wooden furniture provided comfort and style. A gentle breeze carried the scent of blooming jasmine, blended with the rich aroma of freshly brewed tea and the crisp, nutty scent of khakara.

Gautam stood near the balustrade, a porcelain cup of steaming chai in one hand and a piece of khakara in the other. His fingers, heavy with gold and studded with gemstones, gripped the delicate cup with surprising ease. Each ring told a story of successful ventures, shrewd negotiations, and a life of relentless pursuit of prosperity. His attire was equally striking: a meticulously tailored kurta of the finest silk, its subtle sheen catching the light with every movement.

He was on the phone, his deep, resonant voice tinged with irritation as he spoke.

"No, no, this is unacceptable. I won't tolerate delays. Do you understand what that means for our reputation? We've built this empire on trust and efficiency. I don't care for excuses, resolve this immediately."

His words were sharp, each syllable enunciated with a precision that brooked no argument. His displeasure was evident, but beneath the stern exterior lay a keen business acumen that had seen him rise to the top of his trade. The person on the other end of the call was trying to placate him, but Gautam's patience was thinning this morning. He bit into his khakara, the crunch loud enough to momentarily punctuate the conversation. His eyes, sharp and discerning, scanned the horizon as if seeking the solution within the city itself.

"I expect a full report by the end of the day. No compromises. And remember, every minute you waste is money lost."

With a curt nod to himself, he ended the call, by dabbing the iPods in his right ear.

He settled into one of the white cushioned chairs on his terrace, placing his tea and khakara on the intricately carved table beside him. He picked up his phone and began to scroll through the call logs from the previous day. His eyes narrowed as he paused at a few missed calls from unknown numbers, calls he had not answered. He recalled leaving his phone in his Audi for a couple of hours while he spent time with his grandkids on the terrace the previous evening. The memory brought a soft smile to his face, but it quickly faded, replaced by a look of regret.

Gautam Mehta had a morning ritual that he cherished almost as much as his tea and khakara. Every day, along with his copy of the Economic Times, he meticulously reviewed the stack of mail and publications delivered to him on the terrace. This daily routine was facilitated by one of his trusted servants, who would bring him the neatly arranged assortment of posts and newspapers. As the servant approached, Gautam set aside his phone and prepared himself for the next part of his morning. The bundle included a variety of items, but it was the catalogs of jewelry designs and industry magazines that captured his attention.

Gautam immediately called back to the number, recognizing the person on the other end. After a brief but intense discussion,

Gautam disconnected the call, feeling a sense of expectation. The conversation had been to the point, yet filled with significant implications. He pondered the details of their exchange, replaying the key points in his mind. Anticipation coursed through him as he considered the possibilities that lay ahead. The call had ignited a spark of excitement, and Gautam knew that the coming days would bring important developments. He felt a mix of eagerness and readiness for what was to come.

With resolute steps, Gautam walked across the terrace through the French doors leading into his home. His mind was already racing with thoughts and questions that needed to be shared. He needed to speak with his wife, to share the emotions stirred by this unexpected reminder of the past. The terrace, the business calls, the day's plans—all were momentarily set aside as he strode towards their bedroom, the phone clutched tightly in his hand.

CHAPTER TWO

THE CHOSEN SEVEN

The Chosen Seven sat in a circle on damp rocks with a slow-burning fire in the middle that gave them much-needed heat. It was not as if they would die of the cold, but their souls still resided within human bodies. They could still feel all the sensations fathomable for a human body, and yet they were special. The frosty Himalayan winds broke the silence. Darkness stretched around, and only the constellations provided some light to indicate the wide plains and towering mountains surrounding the area. No other living being breathed nearby. A mystical aura surrounded the place. No one had moved an inch since the last full moon "Purnima". The moon was now a thin crescent and was going to disappear the following night, "Amavasya". Time had stopped for them.

The deep meditative state had stopped the aging process. Their breaths came only every few minutes and slowly filled their bodies. This small movement was the only indication of life within them. Each one had a unique body type, but their attire was similar. Their bare upper bodies were exposed to all the elements of nature, while the rest of their bodies were covered with white muslin cloth. Tight skin, flexed muscles, and even skin tone indicated the good health that each of them had managed to maintain. The air in that place must have had something magical in it, providing these seven men with all the essential energy to live and maintain their health.

Another day passed with no movement or sound. As night engulfed the area in darkness with no sign of the moon, uneasiness prevailed on a few of their faces. Creases started to appear on some faces, soon spreading like an infection until they showed on all. The night grew darker, and the constellations disappeared behind the clouds. The wind picked up, and the trees broke the silence. In a coordinated way, all seven opened their eyes, distress, and anxiety evident on their faces. The magical firewood, which had been burning for days without exhausting itself, started to flicker.

Since the dawn of time and life on Earth, death has always been the ultimate fate of all living beings. Though mostly unavoidable, there were a few who have managed to escape it, blessed or cursed with immortality. The quest to evade death and achieve eternal life has been a timeless pursuit for both gods and men. These seven individuals had attained immortality, but with the passage of eons, they had come to see it as more of a burden than a blessing. They had witnessed the passage of countless ages and had experienced everything the world has to offer.

Perched upon a damp rock, amidst the serene stillness of nature's embrace, sat a figure of profound intensity and contemplation. His towering frame, cloaked in the ethereal mist, exuded an air of stoic majesty. Dark as the gathering storm, his complexion hinted at the tempest of emotions churning within. Eyes, ablaze like smoldering embers, pierced through the veils of existence, reflecting depths of resolve and inner fire. Cascading locks, like strands of midnight, framed a countenance etched with the wisdom of ages past, a testament to his journey through the crucible of time. Amidst the tranquility of his meditative repose lingered an enigmatic aura, hinting at mysteries untold and powers veiled beneath the surface. Ashwatthama, an elusive enigma, a figure both revered and feared, as timeless as the eternal dance of creation itself, unfolded his legs and stood. He looked at the southern plains with a mixture of hope and animosity. He was one of the seven guardians of a secret that had been kept beyond time. Five others stood up following Ashwatthama, while one remained in the meditative pose. He was Sage Vyasa.

Cross-legged upon a moss-covered stone, his form radiated a tranquil aura that seemed to merge seamlessly with the verdant landscape. A mask of serene detachment, betraying none of the profound mysteries that churned within his soul. Around him, the air hummed with otherworldly energy, as if the very fabric of reality bent to acknowledge his presence. For in this moment, Sage Vyasa was not merely a man, but a vessel through which the divine manifested, a bridge between the mundane and the mystic. As he sat, his presence served as a reminder of the boundless depths of the cosmos, waiting to be explored by those brave enough to seek its secrets.

The mighty monkey warrior known for his unwavering devotion to Lord Rama and his extraordinary strength and agility, Lord Hanuman, was closely observing the expressions on each of the seven immortals – Chiranjeevis. He sensed that something was bothering Sage Vyasa and others.

"What is it that would have broken the "Dhayan" (meditation) of all the Chiranjeevis, Sage Vyasa ?"

These were the first words that Hanuman uttered other than his love and devotional verse – "Jai Shree Ram".

"Lord Hanuman, there is some force which is trying to take our greatest secret from us. The secret that has kept the balance in this universe. The secret we all know but have not thought about, in the last few hundred years. The secret which can give powers unimaginable, and I am afraid that some nefarious group of humans have found some information which we were hoping to keep as a secret till the end of time" Vyasa broke the silence with folded hands.

"All these years, we have seen many who have intentions to attain the secret but none have ever come close to giving the great Chiranjeevis a concern. What is it that makes them formidable this time?" Hanuman looked at everyone around for some answers.

"Persistence is a very powerful indulgence which, when used in the right way, can help to pursue any goal. Some forces have invested generations to explore and gather information. The accumulation of all the information has resulted in getting closer to the secret" Vyasa responded to Hanuman's question.

After a brief moment of contemplation, Vyasa stood up. He could sense the reason why Ashwatthama was looking towards the southern plain and what he wanted to indicate with his gaze.

"We need to protect it. All the seven elements which are in the mainland need our utmost amount of surveillance. It is time we take up our role of Guardians and make our journey to the locations. Remember that our identities need to be hidden at all cost. Go and mix in the crowd, take professions of this current world and protect your element" Vyasa spoke in a stern voice.

"How do we know if everyone has their element safe and protected? " Ashwatthama looked towards Vyasa and enquired.

"Yes, on that. I have a plan for that. For now, take these and they will help you with all types of communication"

Vyasa gave everyone a small cube, very similar in design to a domino. But each face of the cube had an inscription written on it. The material was as hard as granite with a pale blue color. The surface felt like a polished wood. All the edges of the cube were curved except one, which was prominently sharper than the rest.

Vyasa asked everyone to touch the cube – "Ghan" to their forehead and press the sharp edge on the "Ajna".

Ajna is the third eye chakra of the human body, which signifies the unconscious mind. The third eye is said to connect people to their intuition, give them the ability to communicate with the world, or help them receive messages from the past and the future.

The Ghan started to glow. Vyasa recited,

"Dhruva Sambandh" "Dhruva Sambandh" "Dhruva Sambandh"

The Ghan stopped glowing. Vyasa asked all the Chiranjeevis to open their eyes and take down the Ghan from their Ajna. The sharp edge of the cube had disappeared and had become curved like the other edges. Some kind of connection and communication pairing had happened which was beyond the modern world's understanding. All the Chiranjeevis secured the cubes in their ways.

Vibhishana was born into the illustrious lineage of demons, with a dignified countenance, eyes that reflected the depth of his soul, and a serene demeanor that belied the trials he had faced. His stature exuded an aura of quiet strength, tempered by compassion and empathy for all beings, and went back to his meditative pose on a rock just beside Vyasa. With closed eyes, he was reciting some hymn which was hard to hear. All the Chiranjeevis respected each other's power and rituals, so no one questioned or interrupted the meditation that Vibhishana was up to. Vyasa was very intuitive and had the great power to read body language and understand the emotions they were going through.

Vibhishana is preparing himself for all the obstacles and sacrifices we need to make in the future. He wants to take the blessings from the Cosmos and all the energy available in it. We should wait for the most powerful and eternal source of energy in the universe to give us His blessing before we start our journey to be the Guardians of our elements"

Vyasa was referring to The Sun "Surya Dev". Everyone agreed with the suggestion and returned to their meditative poses and began to visualize the events that might unfold in the future. This practice was akin to the visualization techniques used by ordinary people.

"*Athletes, for example, employ this method before competitions, imagining their opponents and mentally rehearsing their actions repeatedly. This technique helps them prepare for surprises that could impact their performance and outcomes. The better one is at anticipating future events and actions, the more prepared one can be.*

While humans can foresee a few days or months ahead, the Immortals honed their ability to foresee decades and centuries into the future. However, not everything they anticipate becomes reality; events can still diverge from their imagination."

The Chiranjeevis' years of wisdom and close study of human behavior had endowed them with this remarkable power and intuition. This was not something new to anyone. Before any major task or change in the world, they would take blessings and engage in the visualization practice. They would play all the worst-case scenario simulations in their head and try to either prevent them or find ways to mitigate them.

The night sky had started to become more amiable. The cloud cover, which resisted the slight light of the stars, had started to fade away. Huge trees which had seen a few centuries eloped the surroundings, but other than these trees and a few small plants there was no life in the area. Born into the lineage of Prahlada, a king who was known for his righteousness, resilience, and generosity, Bali inherited not only the throne but also a legacy of valor and benevolence. With broad shoulders that had carried the weight of his responsibilities with grace, his demeanor exuded confidence and wisdom, adorned with the markings of a noble leader. His eyes, though kind, held a spark of determination, reflecting his unwavering commitment to his principles. He spoke, looking at the stars.

"We are a few hours away from sunrise"

He took his seat and folded his legs into a yoga position. He closed his eyes and began to invoke Lord Vishnu, the protector of the world, and seek blessings of wisdom and patience to overcome the impending disaster.

"We should leave for our destinations as soon as we take blessing from the Sun God. Have the Trinity Gods blessed us with any information about the events that are going to unfold in the future?" Parashurama's voice resonated with the deep timbre of authority and conviction.

His voice carried the weight of his experiences and wisdom. When he spoke, he commanded attention, drawing listeners into a realm where each word held the power to inspire, instruct, or admonish. Born as the sixth incarnation of Lord Vishnu, Parashurama's story was one of divine purpose and earthly trials. From a young age, he displayed an innate mastery of warfare and combat, earning him the title of "Rama with the Axe." Yet, his skills were tempered by a sense of duty and righteousness that guided his actions.

"The Gods have left the protection and extraction of the elements to all of us. I believe we always have their blessings, guidance, and love. We should do what we feel is the right thing, God will pave the way for us. I agree with Parashurama. We should start early, it will take us some time to get into the real world after so many years, and create an identity for us. We are in the Kalyug, and moral and spiritual values must be on a decline. It's an era of darkness, marked by widespread greed, dishonesty, and conflict. In Kalyug, virtues diminish, and vices thrive, leading to societal decay and spiritual ignorance. Time itself is said to be compressed, with lifespans decreasing and suffering increasing." Kripa shared his wisdom with the group.

As a learned sage and a formidable warrior, Kripa was marked by humility and a deep understanding of the cosmic order. With a calm mind and a voice that brings the experiences of ages, his guidance was sought after by kings and commoners alike. His actions were guided by principles of righteousness, and his presence showed an impression of serenity and inner strength that made him a timeless symbol of virtue and integrity.

The first rays of the Sun kissed the skin of the Chiranjeevis, they all radiated like gold. A clear blue sky and a cold breeze made the morning very pleasant. All the Chiranjeevis opened their eyes and broke their meditative prayer with the warmth of the Sun. They walked through the tall ageless trees to a small stream with a rocky bank. The rocks were all white with not a single spot or crack on them. It seemed the water and rocks lived in harmony here. The water was transparent and clear. The stream had a steady flow, the touch of cold water to the feet early in the morning energized the whole body of the Chiranjeevis. Each of them picked a place in the rocky banks and cleansed their bodies. They offered a small prayer to the Sun God as He would be with them everywhere they go in this world. His blessings would give them the energy to fight evil and to purify their souls if they commit any sins. Each had their way of offering their prayer but ended with the "Surya Namaskar".

"Surya Namaskar is a sequence of yoga poses performed in a fluid motion, paying homage to the sun. It combines physical exercise, stretching, and breath control, promoting strength, flexibility, and mental focus. Each posture in Surya Namaskar offers holistic benefits, fostering physical vitality and spiritual connection."

After taking the blessing of the Sun God, they came back to the same place where they had meditated the last few nights. Vyasa wanted to address the whole group with some of the key things to look out for when they visit the human world.

"We are the Chiranjeevis. Be it a blessing or a curse, we are all here for a reason, to maintain the balance of the world. Each of us is given the responsibility to safeguard and extract one element that's unknown to others. The location and method of extracting the element are familiar to us all. For some cases, we must seek assistance from the Keepers, while in others, we must handle the task ourselves."

"Seven elements, seven places, Seven Chiranjeevis to keep one secret"

After addressing the group, Vyasa took out a Pepal leaf tied around with a red thread. The leaf looked lively and green like it was just plucked out of the tree. It contained a vermilion paste which looked freshly made out of turmeric and ghee. Immortality appeared to have extended to the objects that came into close contact with the Chiranjeevis. Vyasa put out his hand and offered the paste to all. Everyone took a pinch of it and applied it in between their brows. The bright red color paste, after being applied on the forehead, disappeared and dissolved in the Chiranjeevis skin. This was one of the signs of being immortal, anything pure which was offered to them became a part of them. Mortal sinned beings would never be able to experience it. Vyasa tied the leaf and put it back into the dhoti.

Hanuman brought seven bananas and offered them to the group, each Chiranjeevi picked one and enjoyed the ripe sweetness of the fruit. Vibhishana had put a small fire on a rock and offered it to all, once everyone took the blessing, the fire died out in thin air and left no smoke or ash. Bali offered a magical flower to everyone, the scent of it filled the area. All the Chiranjeevis felt and breathed the air with the scent. It vanished as soon as it reached the lungs of all the Chiranjeevis. Kripa offered a sacred hymn to be read from a leaf, it disappeared after each of them recited. Aswathamma offered water and Parshurama offered the head of an arrow to all the Chiranjeevis.

The Chiranjeevis consumed all the items in their entirety, causing them to vanish once the process was complete. This act was both a blessing and a means of mutual protection. A part of them, or a fragment of the blessed items, would forever remain within each Chiranjeevi. Though they would eventually part ways, the collective power of all would continue to reside within each of them.

Vyasa's vermilion paste protected the exterior bodies, the bananas offered by Hanuman gave the energy and physical power to all. Vibhishana's fire kept the Dharma and spirituality burning in each one of them. The scent of flowers would purify the air that the Chiranjeevis were going to consume. Aswathamma's water helped them quench all the worldly thirst within and the arrowhead gave their weapons the sharpness and valor to fight any evil in the world. This unification of power made each one of them a formidable force.

"In Hindu mythology, the Chiranjeevis were seven immortal beings granted eternal life to fulfill divine purposes and uphold dharma until the end of Kali Yuga. Each of them achieved immortality as a boon for their unique contributions and virtues. Ashwatthama, the son of Dronacharya, became immortal after misusing the Brahmastra during the Mahabharata, earning a curse from Lord Krishna to wander the Earth as a cautionary figure. Mahabali, a virtuous asura king, was granted immortality by Lord Vishnu's Vamana avatar after demonstrating humility and devotion by surrendering his kingdom. Similarly, Hanuman, the devoted servant of Lord Rama, received immortality from the gods for his unwavering loyalty, courage, and unparalleled role in the Ramayana.

Vibhishana, Ravana's younger brother, was immortalized by Lord Rama for choosing righteousness over familial ties and aiding in Ravana's defeat. Kripacharya, the wise teacher and elder of the Kuru dynasty, survived the Kurukshetra War and was blessed with immortality for his impartiality and dedication to dharma. Parashurama, the warrior-sage and sixth avatar of Vishnu, earned his eternal life through his mission to restore balance in society by eliminating corrupt rulers. Sage Vyasa, the author of the Mahabharata and compiler of the Vedas, was also made immortal to preserve sacred knowledge for future generations."

The Chiranjeevis started their journey from one of the uncharted realms of our world. Gangkhar Puensum, which stood majestically at the border of modern-day Bhutan and China. The mountain's pristine slopes were blanketed with untouched snow, glistening under the sun like a vast expanse of diamonds. Rugged cliffs and serene glaciers intermingled, creating a landscape of stark contrasts that captivated the eye. Wisps of clouds often embraced its summit, adding an ethereal, almost otherworldly aura. A great place to hide and live in nature's wilderness, the Chiranjeevis had made this their home for the last 2500 years. They had traveled into the human world intermittently every few centuries to resolve some imbalance or protect the secret, but once the job was done they would travel back to the Gangkhar.

Hanuman's tail, usually a testament to his monkey god heritage, receded, blending seamlessly with his new human form. His ears reshaped, losing their pointed tips to adopt the round, modest shape of a common man. His powerful voice, capable of reverberating across the heavens, softened into a melodious, reassuring tone. With each step he took, a faint trace of magic lingered in the air, as if the very earth acknowledged his divine presence. As the transformation continued, his mighty Gada (mace) dissolved into the morning mist. As Hanuman completed his transformation, he picked up the pace, expertly maneuvering through the rugged forest paths.

To the mortal beings, he would appear as a humble milkman, kind and dependable. Yet, beneath this simple exterior lay the heart of a hero, ready to unleash his divine strength and wisdom at a moment's notice, should the need arise. Thus, Hanuman, the eternal guardian, seamlessly blended into the tapestry of mortal life, his true identity masked by the mystical magic of his transformation.

He had to travel from Gangkhar to Rameswaram, a distance of around 2400 km towards the south of India. Embarking on a sacred journey from the mystical heights of Gangkhar Puensum to the revered shores of Rameswaram, Hanuman sought the blessings of two significant Hindu temples along the east coast of India. Each temple, steeped in historical and spiritual significance, marked a poignant chapter in his divine quest.

Hanuman's first stop was the Kamakhya Temple in modern Assam, nestled atop the Nilachal Hill in Guwahati. This ancient temple, dedicated to the goddess Kamakhya, a form of Shakti, was one of the most important pilgrimage sites in Hinduism. According to legend, it was here that the yoni of Goddess Sati fell, making it one of the Shakti Peethas. As Hanuman arrived, he was greeted by the temple's red spires rising against the lush green backdrop. The air was thick with the scent of incense and the chants of devotees. He offered his prayers, seeking the goddess's blessings for strength and guidance on his journey.

Continuing his pilgrimage, Hanuman arrived at the Jagannath Temple in Puri, Odisha. This temple, dedicated to Lord Jagannath (a form of Lord Vishnu), along with his siblings Balabhadra and Subhadra, was one of the Char Dham pilgrimage sites. The temple's towering structure, adorned with intricate carvings and the iconic Neela Chakra (blue wheel) atop its spire, was a testament to the architectural prowess. Hanuman, with reverence, paid homage to the deities, seeking their blessings for protection and perseverance.

Finally, Hanuman arrived at his destination, the Ramanathaswamy Temple in Rameswaram. This temple, one of the twelve Jyotirlingas, was dedicated to Lord Shiva. It was here that Lord Rama, with the help of Hanuman and his vanara army, built the bridge to Lanka to rescue Sita. The temple's long corridors, adorned with beautifully carved pillars, lead to the sanctum housing the sacred lingam. Hanuman remembered his beloved Lord Ram and Sita Mata while he gazed at the ocean in front of him, which he had leaped to visit the Lanka. Rameshwaram was going to be his home till the Chiranjeevis were able to complete their task on hand.

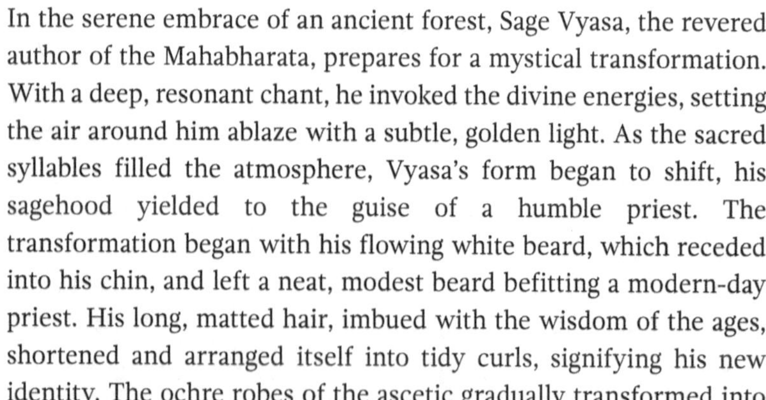

In the serene embrace of an ancient forest, Sage Vyasa, the revered author of the Mahabharata, prepares for a mystical transformation. With a deep, resonant chant, he invoked the divine energies, setting the air around him ablaze with a subtle, golden light. As the sacred syllables filled the atmosphere, Vyasa's form began to shift, his sagehood yielded to the guise of a humble priest. The transformation began with his flowing white beard, which receded into his chin, and left a neat, modest beard befitting a modern-day priest. His long, matted hair, imbued with the wisdom of the ages, shortened and arranged itself into tidy curls, signifying his new identity. The ochre robes of the ascetic gradually transformed into the modest saffron attire of a priest, exuding simplicity and quiet dignity.

Vyasa's eyes, deep wells of cosmic knowledge, softened and adopted a gentle, approachable gaze that speaks of compassion and guidance. His robust, muscular frame became leaner, more reflective of a man dedicated to the daily rituals and duties of temple life. The rudraksha beads around his neck, symbols of his profound spiritual journey, remain but now blend seamlessly with the new persona, exuding an aura of quiet strength and devotion. His sacred thread, a mark of his Brahmin lineage, glowed briefly with an ethereal light before settling into its new form, denoting his readiness to serve as a spiritual guide for the people. The mystic symbols on his skin, barely visible, shimmered once and then faded, leaving only the essence of his wisdom and serenity.

As the transformation was completed, Vyasa stood as a priest, embodying humility and devotion. The forest around him seemed to bow in reverence, acknowledging the seamless blend of mystic power and priestly grace. With a serene smile, he stepped forth, ready to guide and bless those who sought the divine, his true essence concealed beneath the humble exterior, yet ever present in his eyes and heart.

Embarking on a divine journey from the dense forests of Bhutan through the northern plains of India, he visited some divine places each imbued with profound religious and cultural heritage. He visited Bodh Gaya, the place where Siddhartha Gautama attained enlightenment and became the Buddha. This was the place where Vyasa had meditated with deep contemplation, allowing him to connect with the spiritual energies that pervade this holy site. Under the Bodhi Tree, Vyasa had composed The Rigveda, the oldest of the four Vedas which holds immense significance in Hinduism as the foundational text of ancient Indian spirituality and knowledge. It comprised hymns dedicated to various deities, praising their virtues and powers. The Rigveda serves as a key source for understanding early Vedic culture, cosmology, and rituals. It introduced fundamental concepts of Dharma (duty) and Yajna (sacrifice) that underpin Hindu philosophy. Additionally, its rich poetic and philosophical content had influenced Indian literature, religion, and philosophy profoundly, making it a cornerstone of Hindu thought and spiritual practice.

He visited the Triveni Sangam – the confluence of the Ganges, Yamuna, and the mythical Saraswati rivers. Situated in the modern Prayagraj, Vyasa took the opportunity to perform rituals and bathed in the sacred waters. The Sangam is revered as a powerful place of pilgrimage, embodying the confluence of physical and spiritual realms, deeply ingrained in Hindu cultural and religious practices.

Finally, Vyasa's journey culminates in Varanasi, situated on the banks of the Ganges. Vyasa would help some souls reach moksha as he served as a priest who performed the cremation rights. He reached the place and found an ashram to dwell in and serve the people while he was on the lookout to protect the secret.

Bali closed his eyes, feeling the magic seep into his being, altering the fabric of his existence. The transformation was not merely physical but a profound rebirth, intertwining his immortal spirit with the essence of the fertile soil beneath his feet. His attire faded into the mist, giving way to the simple yet resilient clothing of a coconut farmer. His new clothes were made from coarse cotton, the earthy tones blending seamlessly with the natural surroundings. A simple mundu, a traditional white garment wrapped around his waist, practical and comfortable for the toils of the field. His skin once radiated an unearthly glow, now bore the sun-kissed hue of a man who spends his days under the tropical sun. The immortal sheen gave way to a healthy tan, rugged and deeply human. His hands showed the calluses and strength of a farmer's toil, capable of climbing tall palms and harvesting coconuts with practiced ease. Bali's body, though still strong and formidable, took on the muscular yet lean form of a middle-aged farmer. His physique, sculpted by years of labor, was a testament to his new life, marked by the relentless rhythms of planting, tending, and harvesting. His face, lined with wisdom and experience, bore a gentle smile, the kind only those deeply connected to the land could possess.

He traveled through the land to the present Bay of Bengal and prepared a small boat with bamboo and jute. He offered a prayer to the Sea God, Lord Varuna, and Vayu, father to Hanuman and God of Wind to help him traverse through the deep seas safely and reach his location near the southern tip of mainland, India. He was blessed with waves helping him sail and wind pushing him safely. It took him a fortnight to reach his destination, present-day Kerala. He off-boarded at night near the Kovallum beach and took an identity as a coconut farmer near the Sree Padmanabhaswamy Temple. His connection to the land was now both mystical and tangible, a guardian spirit in the guise of a humble farmer.

As Parshuram started his journey, he came to his original warrior avatar before he transformed into a human, a mortal being with a new identity as a martial arts teacher. As the warrior sage, Parshuram's presence was both formidable and serene, his divine axe a symbol of his power and his purpose. Clad in ascetic robes, his skin glowed with an ethereal light, a testament to his divine origin.

Yet, this evening, the atmosphere was charged with a mystical energy. The winds carried an ancient melody, a haunting tune that seemed to rise from the very earth. As Parshuram closed his eyes, the melody grew louder, wrapping around him like an invisible cocoon. The magic of the land, ancient and potent, began to weave a spell of transformation. The first sign of change was in his attire. The simple, divine robes began to shimmer and dissolve into the air like mist. In their stead appeared the vivid, practical attire of a Ranapa Nacha martial artist. The new garb, tailored from durable fabric, fits snugly, designed for unrestricted movement. Its vibrant colors and intricate patterns were both functional and steeped in symbolism, embodying the cultural richness of the region. A tightly bound turban crowned the transformation, its ends fluttering in the breeze like banners of defiance and war.

Parshuram's divine complexion deepened to the rich, sun-kissed brown of a seasoned martial artist. His skin now bore the texture and resilience of one who had trained under the harsh sun, each line and scar a testament to countless hours of rigorous practice and battle. His body, still powerful, shifted subtly. The bulky, divine muscles of a warrior god transformed into the lean, sinewy frame of a martial artist. His physique became more agile, his muscles honed for speed and precision rather than sheer strength. Every movement now carried a fluid grace, a testament to his mastery of Ranapa Nacha, a form that demanded both strength and elegance. As the transformation continued, his hands, once capable of wielding divine weapons, adapted to the tools of a martial artist. Calloused and strong, they now held the knowledge of ancient techniques, capable of both teaching and combat. His feet, once accustomed to the celestial paths, felt the earth with a newfound intimacy, grounding him in the reality of his new role. The final touch was in his demeanor. The stern, divine features of Parshuram softened into the wise and approachable visage of a teacher. His eyes, still sharp and penetrating, now held a glint of warmth and understanding. He had become a guardian of tradition, a mentor to those who sought to master the martial arts of their ancestors. As the magical melody reached its crescendo and faded into the night, Parshuram opened his eyes. The transformation was complete. He stood, no longer a divine warrior but a revered martial art teacher of Ranapa Nacha.

He had two sticks with a pedal-like feature to stand on. The stick used in Ranapa Nacha called "Ranapa," was crafted from sturdy bamboo or hardwood, ensuring durability and flexibility. The Ranapa stick was six feet long and was adorned with intricate carvings and vibrant paint, reflecting the rich cultural heritage of Odisha. Parshuram started his journey on foot from Gangkhar Puensum to the foothills of Mahendra Parvat. On his way, he visited the Lord Jagannath temple in Chhatia, Odisha, where the last incarnation of Vishnu, Kalki, is going to take birth to place order in the world.

Parshuram walked gently along the shoreline of Chilika Lake, Odisha, the largest coastal lagoon in India. With each step, he marveled at the tranquil beauty of the shimmering waters, dotted with fishing boats and migratory birds that graced the lake in winter. As he walked, he encountered remnants of old fishing communities whose traditions dated back generations. He paused at the Kalijai Temple on an island within the lake, where myths of the deity Kalijai merged with local folklore. The air carried the weight of stories and the lightness of life.

In the foothills of Mahendra Parvat near the southern tip of the state of Odisha, there was a small town, Paralakhemundi, where Parshuram took his new identity.

The winds of change carried whispers of a calling from the distant shores of Trincomalee, Sri Lanka. With a heart open to destiny, Vibhishana prepared for his transformation. Amidst the sacred peaks, a mystical energy enveloped Vibhishana. His tall, regal form, reminiscent of his royal lineage in Lanka, began to shift. His attire, once grand and befitting a king, transformed into simple, yet sturdy, garments suitable for a cook. His skin, bronzed and radiant with the glow of immortality, took on a more human hue, reflecting the complexion of a man accustomed to working in a kitchen. The divine aura that surrounded him softened, allowing him to blend seamlessly with the mortal world. His hands, once powerful and adorned with royal rings, became those of a seasoned cook, skilled and agile, capable of crafting culinary delights with precision and care. His eyes, however, retained their wisdom and depth, hinting at the timeless soul within. The transformation was complete, and Vibhishana was ready to embark on his journey to Trincomalee.

Leaving Gangkhar Puensum, Vibhishana traveled through the rugged terrain of the Himalayas, descending from the heights of snow-capped mountains. His path led him through lush valleys and dense forests, each step bringing him closer to his new purpose. The journey was both physical and spiritual, a pilgrimage that reminded him of the transient nature of existence and the enduring spirit of service. Vibhishana crossed the borders of Bhutan into India, moving through the bustling cities and serene villages of West Bengal and Odisha. In each place, he found moments of reflection and inspiration, absorbing the diverse cultures and cuisines along the way. The journey was long and arduous, but Vibhishana embraced it with patience and humility, understanding that every step was a part of his transformation.

Finally, he reached the coastal state of Tamil Nadu. Here, the scent of the sea grew stronger, and the promise of his destination beckoned. He traveled along the Coromandel Coast, following the ancient trade routes that had connected India to Sri Lanka for millennia. The waves of the Indian Ocean carried him across the Palk Strait, and as he approached the shores of Trincomalee, he felt a profound sense of homecoming. Trincomalee, with its stunning natural harbor and rich history, welcomed Vibhishana with open arms. He found solace in the city's ancient temples and vibrant markets, blending in with the local community. Embracing his new identity, Vibhishana became a cook at a small, bustling eatery near the Koneswaram Temple.

A mystical aura surrounded Kripa, initiating his metamorphosis. He now wore a white dhoti and kurta, made from the finest cotton, symbolizing purity and simplicity. A shawl, draped gracefully over his shoulders, signified his new role as a healer and scholar. Kripa felt a profound stirring within his soul. The winds seemed to whisper a new destiny, calling him to a life of healing and care. Kripa's physical appearance subtly shifted. His once muscular frame, honed by years of combat training, softened into a slenderer and more approachable figure, reflecting the gentle touch of a healer. His skin, weathered by the harsh climates of battlefields and mountainous retreats, took on a healthier, subtle glow, indicative of someone who spent time in the natural elements, gathering herbs and practicing medicine.

His hands, which had wielded weapons with precision and strength, now exuded warmth and care, ready to heal and nurture. His eyes, still sharp and wise, now held a compassionate gleam, reflecting his inner transformation from warrior to healer. The divine aura around him mellowed into a comforting presence, one that reassured and calmed those in his vicinity.

With his transformation complete, Kripa set forth on his journey from Gangkhar Puensum to Ujjain, a city renowned for its spiritual heritage and ancient traditions of healing. Kripa's journey was marked by moments of introspection and learning. He visited ancient temples and interacted with sages and healers, absorbing their wisdom and sharing his insights. His travels through India's heartland brought him closer to the common people, understanding their ailments and the natural remedies they relied upon. Ayurvedic wisdom in India, rooted in ancient texts like the Charaka Samhita and Sushruta Samhita, emphasized a holistic approach to health. Practitioners prescribed remedies tailored to individual doshas (body constitutions: Vata, Pitta, and Kapha), promoting balance.

Finally, after weeks of travel and study, Kripa reached Ujjain.

Ashwatthama's form began to shift and change. His hands, once stained with the blood of countless foes, now bore the calluses of a laborer, strong and skilled. His eyes, once fierce and unyielding, now held the quiet resolve of a man who had found solace in the dance of fire and metal. His dhoti transformed into a rugged attire that could withstand the heat of melting metals. Crossing the border into India, Aswatthama traveled through the bustling cities and serene villages of Assam and West Bengal. Along the way, he sought to modernize his blacksmith craft. He traveled to nearby towns, observing advanced techniques and machinery in workshops. Fascinated, he studied modern tools, from electric forges to automated hammers, blending them with his traditional methods. Through books and conversations with skilled artisans, he learned about alloy properties and industrial designs. Their words resonated deep within his soul, guiding him on his path of transformation.

Ashwatthama's path led him through the fertile plains of Gujarat, where the air was heavy with the scent of blooming flowers and the distant murmur of the sea. The sight of the Arabian Sea on the horizon filled Ashwatthama with a sense of anticipation, for he knew that his destination lay just beyond the horizon. Finally, after a few weeks of travel, Ashwatthama arrived in Dwarka, the legendary city of Lord Krishna. Here, amidst the bustling streets and ancient temples, he found a new purpose for his immortal soul.

CHAPTER THREE

SEEKER'S DRIVE

Year 1984

Young Arvind Mishra often found himself immersed in the dimly lit corners of his grandfather's vast warehouse. This sanctuary of books and manuscripts, rich with the scent of aged paper and the whispers of centuries past, was his playground. One fateful afternoon, as a monsoon storm raged outside, Arvind stumbled upon a leather notebook hidden within a false-bottomed drawer in his grandfather's desk. Its pages, brittle and yellowed, were inscribed with a language and symbols he could barely comprehend. As Arvind was trying to inspect the notebook and its meaning, Suryaprasad noticed his eldest grandson engrossed in one corner of his office holding some book. He became curious and went to check on Arvind.

"Where did you find this, son?" Suryaprasad enquired with a calm voice. He didn't want to startle his grandson, which could lead to damaging the notebook.

"I was trying to find glue to fix my kite's tail and was searching the drawers of your table. When I was closing the last drawer, I found the knob loose. To fix it, I rotated it a few times when the side wooden flap came off. I looked inside and found this wrapped in this plastic bag."

Arvind explained the episode with innocence, looking at his Grandfather who was standing beside him.

"What is it? It is not written in Devanagari script."

Arvind, who had a good understanding about scripts and languages of the Hindu religious scriptures, shared his curiosity with his Grandfather.

"This is a book which has all the knowledge passed by our forefathers of the Mishra family. They were all highly acclaimed priests and scholars who have passed their legacy in the form of this text. A lot of it is lost and forgotten, this is the only one I got from my father"

"What type of knowledge does it have?"

"When the Gods had taken human form on earth, they shared knowledge about the way of leading a good life. Most of them are documented in the form of Vedas, Upanishads, The Bhagavad Gita, and so on. But there were a few things which the Gods didn't want to pass the knowledge to the Humans. Supernatural powers, advanced technology which can disrupt the balance of the living world, infinite energy sources, and alchemy knowledge are few of the things which are mentioned here."

"This is so interesting. Did they have any superpowers, like flying?"

"The knowledge is from a few thousand years back, so it is very hard to decipher them. The only way to do it is to accumulate a lot of knowledge by reading ancient scriptures, talking to the scholars, and finding correlations."

He continued with a smile, "And no, we have not yet learned to fly, but we have now airplanes that can take humans from one place to another"

"Give me the notebook, I will keep it safe. When you grow a little older, I will give it to you so that you can decipher it and pass the knowledge to our next generations" Suryaprasad took the notebook from Arvind.

Years passed by, and Arvind became busy with his life, friends, and forgot about the notebook. His days were filled with the typical joys and trials of youth, and his nights were spent in laughter and camaraderie. The shadow of the ancient text faded into the recesses of his mind.

On the evening of Arvind's 16th birthday, he was surrounded by friends, the air buzzing with laughter and the clinking of dinnerware. The party was a lively affair, filled with music, jokes, and the warmth of friendship. As the evening drew to a close and the last of his friends bid their farewells, Arvind felt a deep sense of contentment. Just then, his grandfather entered his room, carrying a small, wrapped gift. Arvind's excitement was palpable as he approached his grandfather, touching his feet in reverence and seeking his blessing. His grandfather smiled a twinkle of nostalgia in his eyes and handed the gift to Arvind.

With eager hands, Arvind tore open the wrapping paper. As the last shred fell away, his breath caught in his throat. There, in his hands, was the ancient notebook of his ancestors he had discovered years before. The sight of the familiar, worn cover stirred a rush of memories and emotions. He looked up at his grandfather, whose gaze was filled with both pride and a hint of solemnity.

"This belonged to our ancestors," his grandfather said softly. "And now, it belongs to you. It is time for you to continue what our ancestors started."

Arvind's heart pounded as he traced his fingers over the intricate symbols on the cover. The notebook, once a mere curiosity, now seemed to pulse with significance. The weight of his family's legacy settled on his shoulders, and the allure of the forbidden knowledge within the pages beckoned him once more. The birthday celebration, with all its joy and laughter, faded into the background as Arvind's mind raced with possibilities. The notebook had returned to him, not as a relic of the past, but as a call to his future. The path of his life, once diverging towards normalcy, now seemed to bend back towards the mysterious and the unknown. And as he stood there, cradling the ancient book, he knew that his quest for knowledge was about to begin anew.

The next few years were very difficult for Arvind. His father met with an accident and succumbed to death in a few months due to multiple organ failures. This event broke Suryaprasad too, seeing his firstborn die in front of him was one of the most feared curses for any parent. He feared this curse might extend and he might have to see his grandchildren's death as well, which made him paranoid for a few weeks. Arvind was devastated by seeing his two strongest support pillars breaking away. He tried to spend more time with his Grandfather for the next few months, to bring him back to normal and make him overcome the grief.

It had been over six months since the demise of Arvind's father. He was sitting on the terrace with Suryaprasad sipping hot tea on a cool November evening.

"Where have you kept the notebook?" Suryaprasad asked in all seriousness.

"Which one?" Arvind was taken by surprise.

"Which one ...., The one I gave to you on your sixteenth birthday"

"I have it in my study desk drawer. Why?"

"The curse can be overcome only by one thing, by skipping the cycle of birth and death. We need to find the secret to becoming Immortals" Suryaprasad laid out his thought.

Arvind looked at Suryaprasad with disappointment. He feared that another episode of mental breakdown and paranoia was grappling with his Grandfather, which might take many more evenings to bring him back to normal.

"Ok. We will discuss it tomorrow. Let us go down and have some dinner." Arvind tried to change the topic.

A few days passed, and Suryaprasad seemed to have recovered and forgotten about the curse and immortality episode. Arvind had started his life back. He visited the college during the day and started to take up the responsibility of the shop and warehouse during the evening hours. He had also started helping his uncle, Dinesh Mishra, the second son of Suryaprasad. Dinesh had opened a printing press a few years back, which had taken off well and had become the primary source of income for the family. The books, scripture, and antique collectibles were still there and Arvind was solely responsible for it. One evening Suryaprasad visited Arvind with a bunch of letters and scripts.

"Arvind, come and sit with me." Suryaprasad patted on the sofa.

"What happened, grandfather? Is everything ok?"

"Yes, don't worry I am ok. I am going to tell you a story which I heard from my father and which he heard from his. Please be patient with me and hear me out."

Arvind took his seat beside his grandfather.

"When I was a few years older than you and started helping my father in this place, he shared this story. Before your father could share it, he passed away and I don't want to delay this any longer" Suryaprasad's voice cracked and his eyes swelled a bit.

"That is ok, Grandfather. Please be strong and share the story. I am curious."

"Do you know the story of "Samudra Manthan" where the Devas and Asuras joined hands to extract the Elixir from the oceans?"

"Yes, I know about it."

After a brief pause, Arvind narrated, "With Vishnu's guidance, they began the arduous task. The devas held Vasuki's tail while the asuras were tricked into believing it was the advantageous end, grasped his head. As the churning commenced, Mount Mandara began to sink, but Vishnu, in his Kurma (tortoise) avatar, supported it on his back. The churning process produced various miraculous items: Kamadhenu (the wish-granting cow), Airavata (the white elephant), Kalpavriksha (the wish-fulfilling tree), and the goddess Lakshmi, who became Vishnu's consort. However, a deadly poison, Halahala, also emerged, threatening the cosmos. Shiva consumed the poison, his throat turning blue, earning him the name Neelakantha. Finally, Dhanvantari appeared with a pot of Amrita. To prevent the asuras from seizing it, Vishnu, in his Mohini avatar, distributed the nectar to the devas, ensuring their supremacy over the asuras."

Arvind recited the full episode in one breath. Suryaprasad smiled exuberating pride in his eyes. Arvind caught his breath and continued.

"After the distribution of Amrita, the devas became immortal, significantly enhancing their power. Enraged at being deceived, the

Asuras attacked the Devas, leading to a fierce battle. Empowered by the nectar, the devas triumphed, restoring cosmic balance. Vishnu's Mohini avatar, who had played a crucial role, disappeared. The gods, grateful for their newfound strength and unity, resumed their roles in maintaining cosmic order."

"Very well, Arvind. This is correct."

Suryaprasad continued.

"But did you know as per some scholars who have studied our scripts, when the war was waged between the Asuras and Devas, the Asuras took the "Amrit Kalash" from Dhanvantari for a brief moment? While the tussle for the elixir was happening, a few drops of it fell into the earth. I have heard another version in the folklore from my ancestors that when Vishnu beheaded the asura Svarbhanu into Rahu and Ketu, a few drops of elixir or Amrit which was in Rahu's throat fell on earth."

"That is fascinating."

"The stories also say when the devas and asuras learned that drops of Amrita had fallen to the earth, they both sought to claim them for themselves. Concerned about these precious drops falling into the wrong hands, some devas requested Vishnu's assistance. To safeguard the Amrita, Vishnu concealed the drops by transforming them into various objects and scattered them across India's mainland. He placed a curse on these objects, decreeing that only when all of them are gathered together would they reform into Amrita, capable of bestowing immortality."

"These are stories, Grandfather. Do you believe in them?"

"Take this. I got this from my father. He told me that this is one of the seven objects which was cursed by Vishnu."

Suryaprasad handed over a scroll to Arvind. The scroll, ancient and weathered, was made of delicate parchment, its edges frayed. Intricate symbols and signs, glowing faintly in ethereal blue, covered its surface. The parchment felt warm to the touch, exuding a subtle aura of power, with golden threads woven into its fabric, hinting at its magical nature.

Arvind was speechless and kept looking at the scroll.

Year 1986

Amara sat on the edge of her bed, the early morning sunlight filtering through the thin curtains, casting a soft glow in her room. Her heart raced as she stared at her landline telephone, eagerly waiting. Today was the day the board exam results were coming out. She had tried to sleep the night before but ended up tossing and turning, her mind was a jumble of anxiety and hope. She didn't have a lot of expectations about her results. Her exams hadn't gone particularly well, and she had prepared herself for disappointment. But her worries weren't about her results. She was anxious about Venkat. Venkat had worked so hard, studying late into the night, sacrificing weekends, and pouring over textbooks. She knew how much these results meant to him, how much he had pinned his hopes on getting into a good college.

A moment later, the doorbell rang. It was Venkat.

"Hey," she answered, trying to keep her voice steady.

"Hey," Venkat's voice was a mix of nerves and excitement. "Are the results out, Venkat?" Amara asked with anticipation

"I... I did it," Venkat said, his voice breaking. "I did it, Amara. I got the marks I needed."

Amara's heart swelled with relief and joy. "Venkat, that's amazing! I knew you could do it!" She felt tears prick at her eyes, a mix of happiness for him and the release of her pent-up anxiety.

"How did you do?" Venkat asked in anticipation.

"Anna has taken my roll number. He has gone to the school to check. I am not very hopeful, you know that. But I am very happy for you." she said quickly.

"Thank you," he said, his voice filled with emotion. "I couldn't have done it without your support. I mean it."

Amara and Venkat's love story began in the seventh standard when a shared laugh over a science project bloomed into a deep friendship. Over the years, their bond strengthened, filled with study sessions, shared dreams, and silent support through life's ups and downs. Though they never explicitly labeled their relationship, their connection was undeniable, a blend of mutual respect, unwavering loyalty, and an unspoken promise to always be there for each other. Their love, subtle yet profound, grew quietly but firmly, rooted in understanding and trust, flourishing into a partnership that neither needed words to define. They both had seen the future together, where Venkat would become a doctor and Amara would be his wife, taking care of the family and kids.

A few years passed, and Amara and Venkat's relationship grew stronger. Their families, aware of the deep bond between them, offered their wholehearted support. Both families agreed that Amara and Venkat would get married once Venkat completed his medical studies. However, destiny had a different end to their story. Medical school had brought about changes in Venkat. The rigorous schedule and new environment began to consume him, and the person Amara knew seemed to drift away. Their once frequent calls and letters dwindled, replaced by long periods of silence and indifference. Amara tried to understand, attributing his behavior to the pressures of medical school, but deep down, she felt a growing sense of dread.

One day, the devastating truth emerged: Venkat was having an affair with a fellow medical student. Amara's world shattered. The man she had loved and trusted had betrayed her in the worst way possible. In the past few weeks, Amara had been ignored by Venkat, who stopped responding to her phone calls to the hostel. She would wait for hours near an STD booth, hoping to receive a call from him, but each time, she left disappointed. One day, Amara spoke with the hostel administrator and got the address to Venkat's medical college and hostel. Determined to confront him, she visited his college alone. Amidst her turmoil, she sought out Rakesh Varma, one of Venkat's close friends whom she could trust.

"Rakesh, where is Venkat? I want to meet him. He cannot just get away with his mischief. I want to meet him one last time and say goodbye"

"It is not a good time, Amara. You should not have come here alone."

"I can manage myself. I have a job now for myself and I am independent."

She waited for him for a few hours. A lot of emotions swelled within her, but she didn't let it control her on the outside. She maintained her composure and decided to travel back to her hometown.

"He should have at least shown the decency to face me and break the news to me. He will regret this decision. Anyways Rakesh, thanks for being a good friend to me."

"Come on Amara. I will ask him to call you. He must be busy with assignments."

"Yeah, ok. You take care, Rakesh, goodbye"

"Wait, I will drop you to the train station."

Amara detached herself from all her friends and family. She convinced her family that she wanted to be independent. She left her hometown, Munnar, and went to Thiruvananthapuram to live alone. She had learned tailoring, and her hobby of craft and design helped her grow a small establishment.

Deep within she had not forgotten or forgiven Venkat. The breakup had left Amara devastated, and she couldn't shake the thought that Venkat had chosen someone else. She started to curse her looks for Venkat's disloyalty. This belief gnawed at her, making her increasingly self-conscious. She scrutinized herself in the mirror daily, obsessing over every perceived flaw. Her self-esteem plummeted, and she became fixated on achieving a beauty that she thought might have kept Venkat by her side.

Amara's desperation led her down an unusual path: the world of occult science. She stumbled upon an old book in a second-hand book store, promising secrets to enhance one's beauty and attract love. Intrigued and with nothing left to lose, she bought it. The rituals and potions described within seemed strange, yet Amara found herself drawn deeper into the practices. She started experimenting with homemade beauty concoctions and performing rituals under the moonlight, convinced they would transform her. Her room filled with the scent of herbs and the glow of candlelight as she followed the book's instructions meticulously. Friends and family noticed the changes in her appearance, but also the haunted look in her eyes, a far cry from the vibrant girl she once was.

The obsession consumed her. Amara isolated herself, driven by the hope that these practices would mend her broken heart and restore her lost confidence. But as she delved deeper into the occult, the line between reality and her desperate fantasies blurred, leaving her in a fragile state, teetering on the edge of sanity.

A few years later, Venkat died under mysterious circumstances. At his funeral, Amara encountered Rakesh, who had gotten married a couple of years earlier and was now practicing medicine in Indore.

"Never thought something like this would happen to Venkat" Rakesh started the conversation with Amara, who was fixated on Venkat's dead body.

"Amara, Amara ... Are you ok?" Rakesh jolted Amara from her trance.

"Yes, Yeah. I am ok. Sorry, I was thinking of something else. You were saying something."

"No nothing. Do you know how this happened?" Rakesh was curious.

"No, I came to know from my mother. She rang me last evening with the news. I was not planning to come, but I had loved him once. Even though he didn't give me a farewell from our relationship, I came to give him a farewell from this world" Amara responded with a hint of happiness and satisfaction in her voice.

"Aaa... yes ok, of course!!!" Rakesh was taken aback by this response.

He dismissed it, assuming it was a shock reaction to their shared history. They paid their last respects to Venkat and began to disperse.

"Do you want to come to my house for a coffee? It is nearby " Amara invited Rakesh to her house in Munnar.

"Sure" Rakesh accepted the invite.

While walking back to Amara's house. Rakesh advised Amara to forget about her past with Venkat. Rakesh spent a couple of hours with Amara, sharing his marriage photos and discussing his work at the hospital. Amara, in turn, talked about her life in Kerala, how she had restarted and was now aiming to open her boutique in Thiruvananthapuram.

"Thanks for the coffee. Not an ideal situation to meet, but good to meet you after so many years. But think about what I said. Forget the past and try to find a partner."

Amara nodded. She had heard the same advice from every person she had met in the last five years and had stopped reacting to them now.

"Amara, I am serious. We are not getting any younger, although you are looking better with age, but as we age, we all need a companion and this is the right time for you. Get a handsome guy while you are younger looking and at good health."

"Don't worry, I am not going to get any older," Amara smirked.

Rakesh laughed at her response.

"No cosmetic product will keep you young like this."

"We will see." Amara concluded.

Rakesh had no clue that Amara's obsession with beauty and agelessness gradually morphed into a longing for immortality. As she delved deeper into the occult, her initial goal of enhancing her appearance evolved. She became fascinated by ancient texts and rituals promising eternal youth. The fear of aging and the desire to escape the pain of her past drove her to seek ways to transcend mortality itself. Her nightly rituals grew more intense, her yearning for an everlasting existence consuming her thoughts. What began as a quest for beauty had become an all-encompassing desire to conquer time and live forever.

Rakesh traveled back to Indore the same evening. He shared the whole incident with Anjali. Things became normal for Rakesh, and after a couple of years, they were blessed with a boy, Ravi Varma. They became a perfect family, with Rakesh's fame growing each day.

When Ravi was five years old, the family traveled to Goa for a vacation. Lazy evenings and sunsets, paired with their favorite food and drinks, felt like the closest thing to heaven. Away from their mundane routine, the family savored each moment of the trip. One day, as Ravi was running on the sand, he suddenly collapsed.

They immediately called in the ambulance and took Ravi to the nearby hospital.

"Everything looks fine; there's no need to worry, Rakesh. But we'll run a few more tests."

Rakesh, despite being a renowned neurologist, found himself clueless to diagnose his son. Dr Alok, a close acquaintance of Rakesh, helped him during the emergency.

Ravi was discharged and they travelled back to Indore the following day. Rakesh and Anjali were seen visibly disturbed over the incident and feared that anything significant had happened to their beloved son. They had not yet broadcasted this mishap to any of their friends or relatives, as they wanted to wait and validate the cause of it. Ravi was equally disturbed over the affairs that had materialized in the last couple of days, a hospital visit would have been a nerve-racking experience for any five-year-old.

"We don't know what happened, he just collapsed while playing on the beach." Anjali was conversing on the phone.

"No, nothing has come in the tests we did in Goa, Rakesh is going to take him today to his hospital and run some more tests. I am very worried, brother. I don't know what has happened to him" Anjali was sobbing and wiping her tears as she sat at the edge of her bed, while she was talking over the phone.

"Who is it on the phone, Anjali? I told you not to panic and spread the news" Rakesh was visibly annoyed.

"I am only sharing it with Arvind Bhaiya. He was worried as we shortened our trip" Anjali responded to Rakesh with a hint of dejection in her voice.

"Tell Bhaiya, not to be worried about it. I will let him know once the results are out." Rakesh tried to console her.

Ravi started to feel better after resting, but felt a lot of weakness in his body. He was finding it difficult to stand or sit for a longer duration of time. Each day Rakesh was growing more anxious, he was not able to find the reason behind Ravi's illness. Rakesh was out of options to diagnose Ravi. He felt the need to do a Genetic blood test. The reports arrived after a day of dreadful wait.

"This can't be right. He is only five. How is this possible? Can you please run the test again, sister?" Rakesh burst out in disbelief after examining the report.

Rakesh's world turned dark when Ravi's report confirmed he had Duchenne Muscular Dystrophy (DMD). The diagnosis indicated a complete or near-complete absence of the dystrophin gene, which was essential for muscle function. There was no cure for DMD, making the prognosis grim. The genetic disorder primarily affected boys and led to severe muscle degeneration, significantly impacting life expectancy and quality of life.

Moments later, Anjali called Rakesh to check on the results. Anjali sat frozen, the phone slipping from her trembling hands as Rakesh's words echoed in her ears—Ravi had Duchenne Muscular Dystrophy. Her heart shattered into pieces, disbelief washing over her. "No, this can't be true," she whispered, tears streaming down her face. She clutched Ravi tightly, his innocent smile oblivious to the storm brewing in her soul. Grief overwhelmed her, a suffocating ache in her chest. How could her lively little boy face such a cruel fate? She pleaded silently, wishing it was a mistake, wishing she could shield him from this unbearable reality. Her world had changed forever.

By the time Ravi was ten years old, he was in the grip of the disease. Rakesh had lost hope and he had gone into an abyss of depression and grief. He had begun missing his hospital duties regularly now and had deteriorated his health significantly.

The family initially struggled, drowning in sorrow and denial. Slowly, they found strength in unity, educating themselves about DMD. Anjali and Rakesh focused on cherishing every moment with Ravi, seeking medical advice, and forming a support network. They celebrated small victories, finding joy in Ravi's laughter and resilience. Over time, acceptance replaced despair, and together, they navigated life with love, courage, and an unyielding hope for brighter days.

After a few years, one morning, the doorbell rang. Rakesh woke up to take the door, expecting either their maid or milkman to be at the door.

"Hi Rakesh"

"Amara, what are you doing here? I mean, Hi. Please come in. How did you know my address? You should have informed me, I could have picked you up" Rakesh blabbered all his thoughts in one single breath.

"Sorry to come unannounced like this, at this hour. I had come to Indore to talk to a few textile dealers for my boutique. I knew you lived here in Indore. Yesterday evening I went to the hospital to meet you, but they said you had taken leave for a few days, so I asked for your address, and here I am. I hope it is not much trouble"

"No, no. Of course not. Come sit. I will call Anjali"

Rakesh went in to get his wife, Anjali.

"Who? What is she doing here, at this time? It is 7 AM, Rakesh" Anjali was annoyed with an unannounced guest at this hour. Anjali came out of her bedroom, wrapping herself with a light shawl.

"Hi !!!" Anjali greeted Amara, with a small hand wave.

"Hi, Anjali. How are you?"

"Hi, Amara. I am good. I had heard about you from Rakesh but I am seeing you for the first time."

Anjali was in awe of Amara's beauty. She didn't look a day older than twenty-one.

"Let me get some tea" Anjali walked into the kitchen and gave a sly nod to Rakesh to follow him.

"You said, she is of your age and was the girlfriend of one of your friends," Anjali questioned Rakesh with a hint of jealousy.

"Yes, I also observed it, she hasn't aged a day. She has reversed aged."

"Please make sure she is gone soon. I can't entertain a guest at this time" Anjali requested Rakesh and went on to prepare some tea.

After a few minutes, tea was served. There was a brief silence in between.

"Where is your son, Ravi? He must be ten years old now" Amara enquired.

"He is still sleeping. He will wake up soon" Anjali responded while looking at Rakesh.

Amara looked at both and kept her tea on the wooden table in front of her.

"Do you want to save your son?" Amara spoke in a stern voice.

Gautam Mehta's office, a modest 200-square-foot space, prominently displayed a large picture of Lord Shiva, Goddess Parvati, Ganesh, and Kartik on its east wall. As his business prospered, Gautam increasingly devoted himself to spiritual practices, believing they were the foundation of his success. Despite being a shrewd businessman, his spiritual devotion was unwavering. Since launching his gems and gold venture four years ago, he had fasted every Monday, crediting this ritual for his growing wealth. For Gautam, there was no looking back. Gautam started each day by offering his prayer to Lord Shiva, in a temple near his office. He offered freshly plucked musk melon tree leaves, "Bale," and flowers to the Shivalinga.

Now in his late forties, Gautam had a son, Vinod, who had just completed his 21st birthday a few weeks back. He was studying a Bachelor of Commerce, completing his final year. He was very keen to join his father's business and make a mark for himself. Gautam had a few more years with him and wanted to keep the reins of his business to himself and guide his sons into the business at a slow pace. Vinod had different plans. Vinod had started to come to the office for the last couple of weeks now, eager to be part of the business and its decisions.

"Who authorized you to take this decision? Why didn't you ask me before ordering these jewelry designs?" Gautam was angry and his temper knew no bounds on Vinod.

"Baba, I thought that ..."

"Here you call me Sir. Who asked you to think here? Now your job is to take orders and learn the ropes of this business. Ask the maker to meet me in the evening"

"But Baba ... I mean Sir. Please look at my ideas, they are going to be hit."

"I have seen them, they are bullshit. Our customers love intricate designs, not plain single-line designs. They don't pay maker fees to us to draw straight lines. Ask the maker to stop the making process immediately. Why am I seeing this after two days? The wedding and festive seasons are going to come, and now I have to deal with this"

Vinod was teary-eyed with this humiliation from his father in front of the full staff. He didn't utter a single word and went back to his desk. This was the first time he received such humiliation in his life. He pulled himself up and called the makers to halt the making process.

"Kaka, please stop making the jewellery designs I had sent. We are revising it and will send a new set of designs by evening." Vinod made a phone call to the factory.

"Ok Baba"

After about an hour, Gautam called Vinod to his cabin.

"Give this to Kaka. Next time, ask me before taking any decisions" Gautam's temper had cooled down.

Vinod nodded and took the designs.

This episode started a rift between the father and son. Vinod started to avoid spending time around his father. Gautam, who was busy building an empire, was not able to fathom the distance in the relationship. Similar events kept happening where Gautam would trash all the ideas Vinod would come up with, and lost his temper often. These frequent humiliations had taken a toll on Vinod's mental well-being. He began spending more time with his new friends, who did not have his best interests at heart.

A few months had passed. One evening while Vinod was hanging around with his friends, one of his friends instigated him against his father.

"You are now twenty-one, boy. If you don't start your own business now, you will always be under your father's shadow. Your father was sixteen when he started, you are already late"

"Yeah, I know"

He kept thinking but didn't respond much to the instigations. These thoughts had started to make a house in his mind. He had started to think about it all the time, but couldn't gather enough courage to speak up to his father.

One evening at the dinner table, Vinod opened up and shared his idea to open a garment business with his father. Gautam was patient. He asked about some details about the business model and investment needs. Vinod realized that he had pitched an unprepared idea. It was more a cry to seek independence than trying to become a businessman.

"Is your intention only to burn my money?" Gautam stringently asked Vinod while he was busy breaking his roti.

There was silence on the table. Gautam's wife was trying to be a peacemaker, but she also knew the absurdness and unpreparedness with which Vinod had come up would not go down well with anyone, especially his father.

"Listen. Complete your studies, take a desk in my company, and draw a monthly salary as your pocket money. Don't think of such things going forward or bring them to me. Learn about the business first."

Gautam refuted and gave a final warning to Vinod sitting at the dinner table.

"Can you give me my share of the property? I will take care of myself after that" Vinod spoke up, gathering all his courage.

Gautam banged the dinner table in anger with his right hand and looked at his wife, hopeless and lost. Vinod left the table, he understood the gravity of the situation. He brought up a topic which was never acceptable in the family.

Gautam Mehta was born to a poor family in a small village. His childhood was a relentless struggle for survival. At the tender age of seven, Gautam had begun working as a newspaper boy, waking up before dawn to deliver papers in his neighborhood. Despite the early hours and the scant earnings, he cherished this job because it allowed him to contribute to his family's meager income. As he grew older, his responsibilities increased. At twelve, he started working as a waiter in a local tea shop. The long hours and heavy trays took a toll on his young body, but Gautam never complained. He used every opportunity to learn from the customers and picked up bits of knowledge about the world beyond his village. It was during this time that he developed a keen interest in business by observing how the shop owner managed his affairs. By the time he was sixteen, Gautam had moved out of his village to take a job as a salesperson in a small electronics store in Surat. Here, his natural charm and persuasive skills came to the fore. He quickly became the top seller, earning praise from his employer. Despite his success, the pay was still not enough to lift his family out of poverty, so he started to work tirelessly, taking up night shifts in a factory. The factory work was grueling and dangerous, but it paid slightly better, allowing Gautam to save a small amount each month.

His big break came in his late twenties when he met an old gem merchant who saw potential in Gautam's sharp mind and unwavering determination. The merchant took him under his wing and taught him the intricacies of the gems and gold trade. Gautam absorbed everything like a sponge, and soon, he was making small deals on his own. His knack for identifying valuable stones and his honest reputation helped him build a network of clients. By his forties, Gautam had established his small shop. Business was slow initially, but his reputation for fairness and quality gradually attracted more customers. Over the years, his business expanded, and he started dealing in diamonds, gold, and other precious gems. His tireless work ethic and keen business acumen paid off, and he became known as a successful merchant.

However, Gautam had little time to enjoy his success. His greed for wealth only grew stronger, which made him dissatisfied and urged him to work more. Despite his financial success, a lingering regret haunted him—he had not been able to enjoy his wealth during his youth. He knew the hardship he had to face to gain the wealth he had, which his sons would never understand. But the rift with Vinod after the dinner table discussion was not forgotten by either of them. After that night, Gautam was not the same, his sadness and disappointment had no boundaries.

Gautam wanted to make amends with Vinod as he grew old, but Vinod had his pride too. One day an astrologer visited Gautam and brought some suitable brides for Vinod's marriage. Gautam took the astrologer into confidence and shared about his relationship with Vinod.

"Visit the Chatur Dhama. Donate some gold and gems to the Gods and ask them to clear your sins. Lord Shiva and Lord Ganesh also had rifts in a great battle." The Astrologer advised.

Gautam took the advice seriously. He embarked on a spiritual pilgrimage to the Chatur Dhama of India, a revered journey encompassing the sacred sites of Badrinath, Dwarka, Puri and Rameswaram.

Gautam started his journey from Dwarka, considered the ancient kingdom of Lord Krishna. Gautam was mesmerized by the temple's grandeur and the confluence of myth and history. It was said that Lord Krishna's grandson, Vajranabh, had built the original temple over the Haran River. A particularly moving moment for Gautam was hearing the tale of Sudama, Lord Krishna's impoverished childhood friend. Despite his poverty, Sudama visited Krishna, who welcomed him with immense love and transformed his life. This story underscored the importance of true friendship, love, and devotion, resonating deeply with Gautam.

Dwarka, also known for its submerged ruins, which legend says disappeared after Lord Krishna's departure. Intrigued by the historical evidence and folklore surrounding the drowned city, Gautam learned about the possibility of many hidden secrets in the drowned city. During his stay, Gautam engaged with local priests and residents who shared tales of lost treasures, believed to still lie beneath the sea. He spent several days sightseeing, meeting fellow merchants in the bustling city.

In the Garhwal Himalayas, Badrinath dedicated to Lord Vishnu was the next stop for Gautam. He felt a deep connection as he approached the temple, surrounded by snow-capped peaks and the serene Alaknanda River. According to legend, Adi Shankaracharya discovered a black stone image of Lord Badrinarayan in the Alaknanda River.

One night, Gautam met a local sage who shared an anecdote about how Lord Vishnu, disguised as a small child, appeared to the sage Vyasa and led him to write the Mahabharata. Gautam visited The Vyasa Cave (Vyasa Gufa), a sacred site located near Badrinath, in the village of Mana. According to legends, it was here where Vyasa composed the Mahabharata. Gautam learned about Vyasa's immortality and was left fascinated by the prospect of immortality.

Gautam's next visit was Puri, located in the coastal state of Odisha, home to the Jagannath Temple, dedicated to Lord Jagannath, an incarnation of Lord Vishnu. Gautam found the place to be vibrant with devotees who were in love, and surrendered, to Lord Jagannath. He met with a few of the locals who shared with him all the fascinating mysteries of the temple. During his stay, he met with an elderly devotee who shared a touching story about the temple's kitchen, the world's largest, where it was believed that food was never wasted. The old devotee also shared about the "Brahma Padartha", a sacred, eternal substance that resides within the wooden idols of Lord Jagannath, Balabhadra, and Subhadra, and how it was considered the soul or life essence of the deities. These miracles, attributed to Lord Jagannath's blessings, impressed upon Gautam the principles of charity and divine providence. The elderly devotee was also en route to complete his Chatur-Dham by paying his visit to the Rameswaram Dham.

"Where are you from?" Gautam inquired to the new acquaintance.

"I am from Berhampur, Odisha. How about you?"

"I am coming from Surat. My name is Gautam Mehta"

"I am Professor Ramkumar Rao. Nice to meet you." Both shook hands with a smile and mutual respect.

In the evening, they visited the sea beach and paid their respects at "Swargadwar," the revered cremation site in Puri believed to be the gateway to heaven. Sitting on the sandy beach of Puri, they watched the sunset and shared their life experiences. Professor Rao spoke passionately about his deep interest in Hindu scriptures, mythology, and stories. Gautam listened with rapt attention, absorbing the knowledge with great curiosity, finding the evening's conversation both enlightening and enjoyable.

Gautam, whose life had always revolved around business, profit, and financial matters, found the spiritual teachings and stories of the gods, which he had known since childhood, fascinating and profoundly insightful.

Both enjoyed each other's company and although there was an age difference of close to ten years between them, they both had a connection. The life struggles of Gautam inspired Rao, he appreciated the hard work and perseverance of Gautam to reach great heights. They decided to take the trip to Rameswaram together.

At the southern tip of India, Rameswaram was renowned for its association with Lord Rama and was the last of the Chatur Dham which they needed to visit to complete the pilgrimage. The Ramanathaswamy Temple, with its magnificent corridors and sacred water tanks, was a major highlight. Gautam learned about the legend of Rama building the Ram Setu bridge to rescue Sita from Ravana. A priest narrated the tale of how Rama, upon his victory, worshipped Lord Shiva at Rameswaram to absolve the sins of battle. Gautam and Rao performed the sacred ritual of bathing in the 22 holy wells within the temple and felt a profound sense of purification and renewal.

Rao had prepared scriptures and questions that he hoped to decode with the help of a local scholar or priest. After consulting with several locals, Rao was referred to Raghavan, a respected priest known for his extensive knowledge of the temple and local folklore. They arranged a meeting with him, and Raghavan graciously invited them to his home near the temple grounds. Rao arrived prepared, carrying a stack of papers and documents, along with a small notepad to jot down notes during their discussion with the priest.

"Namaskaram" With folded hands, Professor Rao and Gautam stood at the front gate of Raghavan's house.

"Namaskaram. Please come in" Raghavan received both of them with folded hands and a smile.

The house was constructed with local materials like brick and wood, providing a cool interior. It consisted of a small veranda where there were three plastic chairs placed in the form of a triangle with a small table at the middle. The walls were decorated with traditional Kolam designs. The courtyard had a Tulsi plant, signifying sacredness. The ambiance was serene, reflecting the priest's humble lifestyle and devotion, amidst the spiritual atmosphere of this holy town.

"Thank you" Rao acknowledged. Both Gautam and Professor Rao took their seat on the plastic chairs.

"Please tell me, how can I be helpful to you, Sir?" Raghavan started the conversation.

"Yes, Sure. I am a Professor in Hinduism Studies and I also study ancient languages. One of my friends found information that can help us prove the theories that we have read and heard in Hindu scriptures or mythological stories. I want to share that information with you, which is relevant more to Rameswaram. If you have any stories, information, scripture, or location that can help us take the study forward, it will be really helpful for us"

Professor opened his bag and took out the folder, which had pictures taken of some scriptures, a mix of original and photocopies.

Before examining the artifacts, Raghavan closed his eyes to offer a small prayer to Lord Shiva.

"I will try my best to help, rest all are in Lord Shiva's hands"

The professor began explaining about the pictures and gave more context and background. He explained the full story that he had heard from Arvind to the Raghvan. Gautam was in awe of these revelations and stories.

"This information is regarding the "Samudra Manthan" episode. As per some legends and stories in the different parts of the country, Lord Vishnu had come down to earth to ensure the "Amrit" drops which had fallen during the rift between the Devas and Asuras did not go into any wrong hands. He had cursed them and transformed them into different items"

Raghavan looked closely at all the articles and heard the stories patiently, but he was not shocked or surprised by the theories made by the Professor.

"I don't know, Sir. I have heard a few stories too. I can tell you that. Seven drops of the "Amrit" had fallen as per some ancient stories, but no one has spoken or depicted about where they could be found. In one of the many stories which were in a positive light to the theories made about the "Amrit" drops, it mentioned that they are protected by the Seven Chiranjeevis. They have taken the responsibility to protect and guard this secret."

"Interesting. But aren't there a few claims that there are more than seven Chiranjeevis?" Professor countered Raghavan's claim of seven Chiranjeevis.

"Yes, you are right. Some stories speak of more than seven. But, we need to believe something and seek for something, but we can never discard anything." Raghavan replied with a faint smile.

"Yes, right. What else can you say about the Chiranjeevis and the items?"

"They are obviously hidden, both the seven Chiranjeevis and the cursed items. If you can identify either, the other should be easy to discover. Some stories say that the items can be the symbols associated with Lord Vishnu like the Shankha (Conch Shell), Chakra (Disc), Gada (Mace), Padma (Lotus), Kastubha mani (Gem), Ananta (Serpent), Vaijayanti mala (Garland) and Srivatsa (Endless Circle mark)."

Professor noted down this piece of information, although he was very well aware of the symbols associated with Lord Vishnu.

"What about the Chiranjeevis?" Professor asked.

"There are so many stories around them and their presence. I know as much as any other person knows. There are many places associated with immortality and the Chiranjeevis, like the Himalayas, Kashi, and even Rameswaram. But I don't want to lead you to any conclusions"

"We are just discussing and curious about their whereabouts. I am sure that we can never find them, they might have disguised themselves as one of us too." Professor smiled, thinking about such a possibility.

"You must have seen many artifacts in the temple's lockers, museums, and local collectors. If you find anything interesting which might tie to this story of ours, will you be willing to help us?" Professor asked Raghavan, he was busy going through the various notes prepared by Rao.

"Of course. If we have the blessing of Lord Shiva, he will help us. I will just be a mere medium to serve Him. Are you ok if I keep some of these notes with me? I would love to study them."

"Absolutely. I can leave a copy of everything with you. Tomorrow I can make photocopies and give them to you"

"Thank you"

Raghavan offered both of them dinner, a simple south Indian meal with Idly with a coconut and peanut chutney. Professor Rao and Gautam could not decline the offer. After a light dinner, they both headed back to their hotel rooms. Gautam was in deep thought and was contemplating all the possibilities based on what he had learned today. Curiosity had dwelled a house in his mind that kept him awake, the whole night.

Next morning, Professor Rao had taken a copy of the notes and came back to the hotel to enquire about Gautam.

"Didn't you have a good night's sleep, Gautam?" Professor Rao asked, observing the swollen eyes of Gautam.

"I couldn't sleep a minute, Professor. I was just thinking about all these stories and possibilities."

Professor Rao laughed at Gautam.

"Welcome to the world of ancient stories and scriptures. We need to take all the information with a pinch of salt, otherwise it will become a nightmare and obsession. Think of them as good stories and forget it."

"Do you think there is any possibility to them?" Gautam asked Professor with a serious face.

"I mean, we are finding pieces of evidence of many mythological events, the occurrence of Ramayana, the Mahabharata, the holy city of Dwarka, and many more. Like the priest said last night, we need to believe something and seek for something, but we can never discard anything."

"Can you give me a copy too?" Gautam requested.

"What will you do with it, Gautam? These are very abstract and encrypted scripts that are very hard to crack or make anything meaningful from them. This is my job and I have spent my life studying about them, that is why I am invested. Don't get into this, if you are thinking of seeking the "Amrit" and immortality."

"Why not?" Gautam responded and laughed at the response.

They went to Raghavan and shared the notes. With a lot of persistence, Gautam also managed to get a copy from the professor and kept it safely in his luggage.

The idea of immortality had started to make a home in Gautam's mind. He looked at immortality as a way to enjoy his life for a very long time, which he never had the opportunity to do. Having spent all his life working and gaining wealth, he wanted to use this idea of seeking immortality as a hobby, which eventually grew into an obsession.

CHAPTER FOUR

HIDEOUTS AND KEEPERS

A few weeks had passed since the Chiranjeevis had arrived at their new locations, each assuming a new identity. They crafted convincing backstories that validated their identities to blend in with the locals. Adopting human forms was not new to them, but the modern world's reliance on technology and existence of digital footprints presented fresh challenges. However, learning new skills was never a problem for the Chiranjeevis, who were blessed with the ability to learn and unlearn at will. To keep things simple and believable, they presented themselves as nomads from rural areas seeking new beginnings. They maintained a humble demeanor and avoided conflicts or actions that might attract attention.

The last time when the Chiranjeevis visited their secret locations was a few centuries back, when there were a lot of demolitions and conquerors happening in the temples. They stayed to ensure some of the secrets that they had been guarding for ages didn't fall into the wrong hands, which could create an imbalance in the universe. The temples had always been one of the safe places for the Chiranjeevis to hide any secret. When they found that it was safe, the Chiranjeevis identified a few local families who could be trusted in the safekeeping of the sacred elements. Although these families' "Keepers" never revealed the secret, a thorough back story was weaved around it.

The Chiranjeevis meticulously scrutinized the Keepers, thoroughly examining each family member and their family history before entrusting them with such a crucial task. Every few decades, the Chiranjeevis would relocate the elements and appoint new Keepers to mitigate any risks. The elements were never kept in direct contact with the Keepers but were stored in a secure location accessible to them. The Chiranjeevis provided the Keepers with motivations such as wealth, prestige, or power, ensuring their steadfast loyalty to the task at hand.

Hanuman disguised himself as a milkman named Amit Vikram. He purchased a few cows and buffaloes from a nearby village and rented a small space to start his own business, allowing him to blend in with the locals. He took orders from local sweet shops and temples to take orders for milk, ghee, and cottage cheese. Thanks to the high quality and authenticity of his products, he quickly built a steady clientele. He also began delivering milk daily to several households, including a group of priests. After a couple of weeks, he approached the family of one of the Keepers, who had been serving the temple for generations. Early one morning, Amit Vikram arrived at the chief priest's house.

"Namaskaram, Guru ji" Amit greeted the Chief priest of the temple.

"Namaskaram, Son. How are you doing today?" The priest greeted back.

"I am doing well. Guru ji, do you have five minutes? I wanted to ask you something."

"Yes, Son. Tell me, what can I do for you?"

"My father gave this to me and asked me to show it to you. He said you would understand its meaning." Amit shared a scroll with a script written in Brahmi to the Priest.

"Your father gave this to you." The priest spoke while he scanned the scroll.

"Yes, Guru Ji"

The priest then looked up to the Sun and folded his hands offering a small prayer.

"Your ancestors had been very kind to us. Our family a few generations back was in ruins, but thanks to your great-grandfather who took us under his wing and gave us the direction to serve the Lord, in return, they had asked us to guard your family's belongings. I am pleased to see that I have been chosen to repay the debts for my ancestors.

Come at 10 PM at the west gate of the temple. I will wait for you. Come in a white Dhoti so that you look like a priest."

"Ok, Guru ji. Thank you."

At 10 PM, Amit stood at the west gate. The priest unlocked a small iron gate and allowed him into the temple. By then, most of the townsfolk were either fast asleep or preparing to retire for the night.

"Follow me." The priest told to Amit.

Nestled within the sacred precincts of the Rameswaram temple laid a hidden chamber, known only to a select group of trusted priests. This chamber shrouded in secrecy, housed an ancient safe that had been concealed from public knowledge for centuries. The existence of this safe was a closely guarded secret, passed down through generations of priests who have sworn an oath of silence. Its location, masked by layers of architectural ingenuity, was known only to these few guardians who ensured its security and sanctity. The hidden chamber was accessible through a labyrinthine passageway that wound beneath the temple's sprawling structure. This passage was cleverly concealed behind a nondescript stone wall, indistinguishable from the surrounding temple architecture.

They both reached the wall.

"Can you please turn around?" The priest requested the innocent-looking Amit. Only the priests knew the precise mechanism—a specific sequence of pressure points that, when activated, caused the wall to slide open, revealing the entryway to the chamber.

"Come in" The priest directed to Amit after completing the unlocking process.

Inside this chamber, the air was heavy with the scent of aged sandalwood and incense, remnants of ancient rituals performed to consecrate the space. The safe itself was an imposing structure, made of thick iron plates and reinforced with mystical symbols etched into its surface. These symbols were believed to be imbued with protective spells, and serve as an additional safeguard against any who might attempt to breach its contents. Once the safe was visible, the priest asked Amit to wait in the passage.

"I cannot allow you to come inside the vault. Please wait here"

The safe's exterior was adorned with intricate carvings, depicting scenes from Hindu mythology, each telling a story of divine protection and celestial guardianship. At its center, a large, ornate lock required not just a key, but the recitation of a specific mantra known only to their guardians. This dual requirement ensured that only those with the deepest knowledge and purest intentions could access the treasures.

Within the safe lay a collection of priceless jewels, artifacts, and ancient scriptures that had never been revealed to the world. The jewels, some of which were said to be gifts from kings and emperors who sought the blessings of the temple's deity, sparkled with an otherworldly brilliance. Each gemstone was believed to possess unique properties, imbuing the wearer with various forms of spiritual and physical protection. The artifacts, meticulously preserved, include ornate statues, ceremonial weapons, and relics from bygone eras, each telling a story of devotion and divine intervention. Among these treasures were ancient scriptures, written on fragile palm leaves, that contained esoteric knowledge and wisdom passed down through millennia. These texts, considered too powerful and sacred for public dissemination, were studied only by the most learned and devout priests. The guardians of this hidden safe dedicated their lives to protecting its secrets, ensuring that its contents remained undisturbed and continued to radiate their sacred power.

After a few minutes, the priest came back while Amit was sitting patiently in the passageway. The priest came back, perspiring and struggling to catch his breath.

"It is not there, Amit. I don't know who would have stolen it or misplaced it". The Priest was visibly disturbed.

"How is it possible, Guru Ji, no one knew about the artifact except our forefathers. Has there been any activity around this safe or someone who might know about it?". Amit asked the Priest maintaining a calm posture.

"Let us go out now, I need to think about the possibilities" The priest wanted some time to clear his mind.

They both returned out and left the temple premises. There was a large tree nearby where they both took a seat.

"A few years back, I was not doing very well health-wise and had shared about this secrecy with my elder son so that he can take the knowledge forward."

"Ok, do you think your son would have ..."

"No, absolutely not. He is not a very clever fellow, but he is not a thief. But thinking of the thief, he had a friend who was guilty of stealing some artifacts from the temple."

"Do you think he knew about this safe? Was he charged for stealing from this safe?"

"He was accused of stealing from the safe and was caught one night by a senior priest. The priest found him holding a shiva linga, and rumors circulated that he had confessed to the police about attempting to steal it. However, after his release, he firmly maintained that he had been falsely accused by the priest."

"What is his name? Where is he now?"

"His name is Raghavan. He had to serve jail for a few years and now he has a small shop selling artifacts and shells near the beach"

Amit returned home, bearing bad news for the Chiranjeevis. He needed to inform his fellow Chiranjeevis about the situation. He recalled that Vyasa had provided each of them with a Ghan. Touching the Ghan to his forehead, he recited, "Dhruva Sambandh." The Ghan began to glow and blink, and after a few seconds, one side of the cube emitted light. Amit touched the illuminated side and heard Vyasa's voice in his head.

"Pranam Lord Hanuman, is everything alright?"

"Pranam Guru Vyasa, the element is missing"

Parshuram arrived in Parlakhemundi, a southern town in present-day Odisha, under the guise of Satya, a dance teacher specializing in the martial art of Ranapa Nach. Upon his arrival, he visited the local art and culture community center to inquire about any available teaching positions. Although there were no immediate vacancies, the community graciously sheltered him. Satya was delighted by the warm reception he received from the community members, who invited him to their homes for daily meals and treated him with respect and affection.

As the festive season approached, the elders in the community decided to utilize Satya's skills to train some of their dance students to perform for the local politician. In return, they offered him shelter and a weekly salary. Despite the job being temporary, Satya was pleased to connect with the locals and establish his own identity. On several evenings, he performed the art form for the community members, leaving them in awe.

Satya began searching for the keeper family, whose ancestors had lived in Parlakhemundi and served under the Gajapati kings. When he inquired with the locals, he discovered that the family had left the town long ago. Heartbroken, Satya realized he needed to prepare a new keeper family before leaving. He knew the location where the secret item had last been hidden by him and a member of the keeper family over four centuries ago. Determined, he decided to visit the place immediately.

Satya stood at the edge of the dense forest with a small bag and a torch, the sound of Gandahati Waterfall grew louder with each step. The air was thick with the scent of damp earth and wildflowers. Sunlight filtered through the canopy, casting dappled shadows on the forest floor. As he approached the waterfall, the mist enveloped him, cooling his skin and heightening his senses. The waterfall, a magnificent curtain of water tumbling over jagged rocks, concealed the entrance to the hidden cave. Satya's heart raced as he recalled the lore: "Behind the falls, where the elephant rests."

He carefully navigated the slippery rocks, feeling the powerful surge of water spray against his face. Hidden behind the cascading water, he spotted the moss-covered boulder that bore the faint engraving of an elephant—a marker left by Parshuram himself. With a deep breath, he squeezed through the narrow gap between the rocks and entered the dimly lit cave. Inside, the sound of the waterfall was muffled, replaced by the soft drip of water from the cave's ceiling. His torch illuminated the ancient, rugged walls adorned with stalactites and glistening minerals. At last, he reached a small chamber, its entrance partially obscured by overgrown vines. With a sense of reverence, he cleared the foliage, revealing a stone platform at the center of the room. There, covered in a thick layer of dust, lay the treasure chest, exactly as he had left it.

There were many symbols engraved on the treasure chest, the Conch, Trisul, Mace, Axe, Lotus, and a leaf. Parshuram closed his eyes in devotion and pulled out a key in the shape of an axe from his pocket. He pushed the key into the axe engraving and the treasure chest started dismantling and opened. A fresh pink Lotus with a stem laid inside the chest, the flower had a slight glow which reflected in his eyes. There was a sense of relief in his face after confirming the safety of his element.

As he sat back on his heels, he felt a profound sense of fulfillment. With a silent vow to protect the ancient secret, he retraced his steps, the roar of the waterfall guiding him back to the world outside. The treasure of Gandahati Waterfall remained hidden, its secrets safeguarded, waiting for the right moment to reveal its ancient mysteries again.

He traveled back to Parlakhemundi and settled on his thin mattress to get into a deep slumber. He needed to find a worthy keeper in the nearby area and inform about the safety of the element to the other Chiranjeevis. As he was thinking about them, he heard a familiar voice in his head, which spoke to him, it was Sage Vyasa using the Ghan to communicate with Parshuram over telepathy.

"Lord Parshuram, one of our elements is missing. We are trying to find it and track the people involved. I wanted to let you know about this mishap." Sage Vyasa spoke with a voice of authority engulfed with disappointment.

"O Sage Vyasa, I am very sad and concerned to hear this news. But don't worry, I have checked mine and it is safe. So, we do not need to worry much as with even one missing piece, the other pieces will not be of much value." Parshuram tried to console Vyasa.

"I agree. I am very glad to hear. I am going to check my element tomorrow. It gives me some respite that one of our elements is safe. I will let you know once others inform me."

Parshuram and Vyasa conversed without uttering a single word. The Ghan was one example of the advancement of technology that the ancient civilizations had. The modern-day technologies were still amateur in front of the ancient ones.

In the lush, verdant landscape of Kerala, under the clear morning sky, a coconut farmer named Ramesh began his daily routine. Bali, the mighty king had taken the new identity wholeheartedly. Having leased a few acres of coconut farm from an elderly couple, he took great pride in his work, knowing that his efforts would help the old couple maintain a good livelihood.

The couple, Mr. and Mrs. Nair, watched from the verandah of their modest home, their faces etched with gratitude and relief. Ramesh approached a tall coconut tree, its rough, fibrous trunk reaching high into the sky, crowned with a burst of green fronds. With practiced ease, he tied a sturdy cloth band, known as a "thorthu," around his feet to grip the tree. He wrapped his hands around the trunk, feeling the familiar texture of the bark, and began his ascent. His movements were fluid and confident, each step took him higher into the canopy.

The sound of rustling leaves and the occasional call of birds punctuated the morning air. As he climbed, Ramesh's mind wandered to the couple's stories of the farm's history, the many harvests they had seen, and the changing seasons. Each tree held a part of their legacy, and he felt honored to be a part of it. Reaching the top, Ramesh paused to catch his breath, looking at the panoramic view of the surrounding countryside. The farm stretched out below him, a patchwork of green dotted with the rounded forms of ripening coconuts. He deftly used his sickle to cut the coconuts from their clusters, letting them fall with a thud onto the soft ground below, where they were collected into a pile.

Mr. Nair shuffled over to help gather the fallen coconuts, his age-worn hands moved with care. Mrs. Nair brought out a pot of freshly brewed tea, the steam rising invitingly. They shared a quiet moment of understanding, a reflection of their partnership and the steady rhythm of life on the farm. As the sun rose higher, Ramesh climbed down, his morning's work nearly done after gathering coconuts from more than a dozen trees.

"Thank you for the tea, Sir. It rejuvenates me after a couple of hours of hard work" Ramesh shared his gratitude to the old man.

"No problem, Son. This is the least we can do for you. You have been so kind to lease this farm from us at such a good rate, but never let us feel that way. You have become like our son"

The old man responded with a smile.

"Ok, I should leave now. I need to sell these in the market. Do you need anything for the house from the market? I can bring it for you while returning."

"No, Ramesh. We are good for today. Thanks for the offer"

Ramesh took off on a bicycle, tying all the coconuts to each side of it. The bicycle was also leased by him along with the farm from the old couple. He tried to sell the coconut wholesale at a lower rate and get himself some free time, but on certain days he didn't get a good price so he preferred selling to the customers in front of a temple or park.

He had been trying to locate a family who created stone sculptures for over two weeks. This family was one of the renowned rock sculptors in the 15th century. During that time, the Sree Padmanabhaswamy temple underwent major renovations under the rule of the Travancore royal family. These renovations included the reconstruction of the temple's sanctum sanctorum, the construction of the long corridors, and the addition of other architectural features that enhanced the temple's grandeur. After some search and investigations, he discovered the location of the family. Their warehouse was located on the outskirts of the city.

Ramesh immediately planned to visit the warehouse without delay. He needed guidance and help from the keeper to locate the secret element due to the vast amount of construction and renovations that had occurred over the last few centuries. Understanding the complexity of the changes made to the area, he realized the keeper's knowledge was crucial. With a sense of urgency, he set out to find the warehouse, hoping to reconnect with the keeper's family. Their ancestral knowledge and familiarity with the historical transformations were essential to uncovering the hidden element, which had been concealed for generations.

"Namaskaram, Can I meet the owner of this warehouse?" Ramesh reached the warehouse and requested one of the craftsmen.

After a few minutes, a strongly built man in his sixties emerged. His salt-and-pepper hair was neatly combed, and he was impeccably dressed.

"Namaskaram, what can I do for you, Sir?"

"Do you have five minutes? I wanted to discuss this with you alone" Ramesh responded with folded hands.

"Sure, Sir. Come in, we can go to the back side where there is no one"

"Was your family the main craftsmen who renovated the Sree Padmanbhaswamy temple in the 15th century?"

"Yes, Sir. How did you know?"

"My ancestors were actively involved in the renovation of the temple during that period. My grandfather often spoke about it with pride, sharing stories about the remarkable craftsmanship that went into the work. He once mentioned that one of the sculptures created during that time holds something extraordinary—a hidden significance. Have you heard anything about the Mukulakara Mandapam and the presence of the Kastubha Mani embedded in one of its sculptures?" Ramesh explained.

"At last, you've arrived. This is a debt we've long wanted to repay to your family. I'm well aware of how your ancestors supported mine during those times. I'll take you to the place tomorrow. Meet me at the Mandapam at 3 PM, when the crowd will be thinner."

In the serene and dimly lit Mukulakara Mandapam, where intricately carved granite pillars stood as silent sentinels, there existed a secret known only to the temple's chief keeper, Anandan. For generations, his family had been entrusted with safeguarding the temple's secrets, including the hidden gem within one particular pillar. This pillar was indistinguishable to the untrained eye and stood near the entrance of the mandapam. Its surface was adorned with exquisite carvings of deities, mythical creatures, and intricate floral patterns. The secret lay in a seemingly innocuous lotus flower carved into the midsection of the pillar. The petals, meticulously detailed, concealed a small, cleverly disguised compartment.

Anandan had learned of the gem's existence from his father, who had learned it from his father before him. The knowledge was passed down through a whispered tradition, along with the key to its retrieval—a precise combination of pressure points and subtle movements. His fingers, calloused from years of temple service, traced the familiar grooves of the lotus flower. With a series of gentle, deliberate presses on specific petals, he activated the ancient mechanism. The center of the lotus began to shift, revealing a hidden compartment just large enough to hold a small, velvet-lined box.

"How come this is empty? I had checked it a few months ago." Anandan was shell-shocked by the revelation.

"Why did you open it without anyone in our family? Did you forget the promise that it should only be opened when someone from my family is present? Only if you are trying to pass the knowledge to the next generation, you are allowed to show the procedure. Were you showing it to your son or daughter?"

"Yes, I know. My father had shown me a long time back. Before showing it to my daughter, I wanted to check again if I recall correctly. But I never touched the box, I had only opened the compartment and closed it again. I know about the curse of opening and seeing the item within it. And after that, I didn't get the chance to share the knowledge with my daughter"

"Please tell me the details. Which day and when were you trying to do this? Was anyone around you?" Ramesh was visibly disturbed.

"Let me think. It was after the Alpasi festival. I had brought my daughter and a few of her friends to the temple."

"Who were they? Do you know them? Did you open in broad daylight in front of them?"

"No, not in broad daylight. I had special permission so we got in at 5 AM when it was closed for other devotees. When the kids went inside, I came here and checked it. I am sure no one was there near me"

"How many friends and who were they?" Ramesh questioned.

"My daughter, along with two friends, Kalpana and Amara. Kalpana is her childhood friend. Amara became her friend a few years back."

"Where do they live?"

"I don't know that, but Amara has a boutique shop somewhere in the town named "Shanti" and Kalpana's family is a neighbor to us. After marriage, Kalpana has settled in another part of the town."

Bali returned with disappointment and anger. He controlled his temper in front of Anandan.

"We should have kept the elements with us throughout, it is never safe with these keepers" He spoke to himself.

He used their covert communication channel to share his disappointment with Sage Vyasa.

"Sage Vyasa, the gem is missing"

In the ancient city of Ujjain, nestled within a quaint and timeworn neighborhood, stood a small thatched house, a relic of bygone days. The house, with its mud walls and sloping thatched roof, was surrounded by a modest garden. Here lived Kripa, an old man whose wisdom was as deep as the roots of the ancient tree that shaded his abode.

Kripa, with his silver hair and deeply lined face, embodied the serenity and patience that came with age and experience. His eyes, though clouded with time, still sparkled with a keen awareness and profound knowledge. Draped in a simple cream-colored dhoti and a faded brown kurta, he moved with deliberate grace, each step measured and meaningful. Inside his humble dwelling, the air was filled with the rich, earthy aroma of various herbs and spices. Shelves lined with jars of dried leaves, roots, and powders spoke of Kripa's lifelong dedication to Ayurveda. A low wooden table, worn smooth by years of use, held a small stone grinder and a mortar and pestle, essential tools in his craft.

He picked neem and tulsi which were revered for their healing properties. With steady hands, he ground the dried leaves into a fine paste, the rhythmic motion of the stone grinder a soothing sound that blended with the early morning chorus of birds.

"Baba, Namaskar" A young man in his mid-twenties knocked at the open door.

"Namaskar, come son. I am almost done with the medicine. How is your daughter now?" Kripa greeted with genuine concern in his voice.

"The fever has gone down, but she is having a cough and throat pain along with the blisters on her skin"

"Give this to your daughter, half a teaspoon three times a day with a little honey, and apply this paste on the skin blisters." Kripa gave a powder and a paste wrapped in a leaf.

The young man left a twenty rupee note beside Kripa and exited with folded hands.

Kripa had started living in Ujjain for a few weeks since his arrival from the mountains in Bhutan. He didn't waste a minute on his arrival, Kripa made his way to the revered cremation ground. The hallowed place, steeped in tradition and reverence, had been tended to by the same family for generations. Their duty, a solemn and sacred one, was to aid in the final rites of the departed.

As Kripa approached, his presence was marked by a serene dignity. The flickering light of funeral pyres cast dancing shadows upon his weathered face, highlighting the lines etched by years of wisdom and experience. He sought the head of the family, a man equally marked by the passage of time and the weight of his responsibilities. The two men greeted each other with mutual respect, their eyes reflecting a shared understanding of life's impermanence. Kripa reached into the folds of his dhoti and carefully retrieved a small object. It was an ancient arrowhead, fashioned from copper, its surface worn smooth by the passage of time. The old healer's hand trembled slightly as he held it out for the other man to see.

"This arrowhead," Kripa began, his voice a low murmur, "is part of a relic that has been in my family for generations. It is said to possess great historical and spiritual significance. I believe your family might hold the remaining piece."

He nodded slowly, a glimmer of recognition in his eyes, and motioned for Kripa to follow him. Together, they walked in the middle of the night through the narrow lanes of the town. They approached the Siddhavat tree, a towering presence that had witnessed countless generations pass beneath its ancient boughs. The tree, sacred in Hindu mythology, was said to be imbued with mystical powers and ancient secrets. The head of the family pointed to one of the massive roots, which bore intricate carvings and symbols from Hindu mythology. These signs, almost hidden by the gnarled bark and the passage of time, seemed to pulse with an otherworldly energy. Kripa's eyes widened with recognition as he observed the unique features of the root.

"This is the spot," the head of the family said softly, indicating a specific point on the root. Kripa nodded, holding the copper arrowhead with a steady hand. He approached the root and, with a precise motion, punctured the designated spot. A faint click resonated through the air, and the root seemed to shudder slightly. Slowly, a small compartment began to reveal itself, hidden seamlessly within the tree. As the compartment opened, Kripa peered inside, his breath catching in his throat. Hidden within was a small artifact, glowing faintly with an ancient aura. It was a tiny, intricately carved Chakra, crafted from an unknown, shimmering material.

Kripa carefully took the small, intricately carved chakra from the compartment beneath the Siddhavat tree. He had recently received urgent news from Vyasa: the elements associated with Hanuman and Bali had been lost. Vyasa had instructed everyone in their group to retrieve these vital elements from their hiding spots and keep them safe. Kripa understood the gravity of the situation. Vyasa also emphasized the need to release the keeper families from their ancient duty of guarding these secrets. It was time for a new generation to take up the mantle of protection.

With the chakra now in his possession, Kripa felt the weight of history and responsibility. He nodded to the head of the family, a silent promise that their long vigil was honored and complete. As he departed, he carried with him not just the artifact, but the collective legacy of their shared guardianship.

Ashwatthama, cloaked in the shadows of dusk, approached the bustling fishing village near the ancient city of Dwarka. His eyes, gleaming with determination, scanned the crowd until they settled on an old fisherman mending his nets by a modest hut. Ashwatthama strode forward, his imposing presence casting a long shadow. In the last few days, he had been following and observing the fisherman.

"Namaste, Sir," he greeted with a respectful nod. The fisherman, startled, looked up from his work. "I need your help. Take me to the deep sea on your next fishing expedition and wait for my return. In return, I will repair your house free of charge."

"How did you know that my house is broken?" The old fisherman was surprised.

"I have been checking on you for the last few days. I have the skill and energy to fix your house and you have the boat to take to my destination."

The fisherman, skeptical but intrigued, glanced at his dilapidated hut and then at the imposing figure before him. "Why should I trust you? Many people have come to me and promised me many things, but most of them have only exploited me."

"Ok. Let me start fixing your house, will that make you trust me?". Ashwatthama said in a firm voice.

Ashwatthama's firm voice and the sparkle in his eyes convinced the old fisherman that he could be trusted. The unwavering confidence in his tone and the genuine glimmer of sincerity in his gaze left no room for doubt, and the fisherman felt reassured by his presence and intentions.

Convinced by the earnest plea and the promise of a better home, the fisherman nodded. "We leave at dawn. Prepare yourself."

As the first light of dawn kissed the horizon, Ashwatthama boarded the modest fishing boat. The fisherman rowed them into the depths of the sea, where the sky met the water in an endless embrace. "I'll wait here," the fisherman said, as he watched Ashwatthama dive into the depths, his figure disappearing beneath the waves, a silent promise lingering in the salt-tinged air. The submerged ruins of Dwarka slowly emerged from the murky depths, ancient stone structures covered in coral and seaweed, standing as silent sentinels of a bygone era. Ashwatthama navigated through the labyrinth of pillars and archways, his heart pounding with anticipation. But as he approached the hollow, his heart sank. The space where the mace should have lain was empty, its absence glaringly obvious amid the undisturbed sediment. Ashwatthama's fingers traced the contours of the hollow, hoping against hope that his eyes had deceived him, but the truth was undeniable—the mace was gone.

Ashwatthama observed that many things had been disturbed in the submerged location. Although the large pillars and rock structures remained intact, the smaller items were missing. He noted the absence of these objects, which left the once complete scene now appearing incomplete and disordered.

Desperation and frustration welled up within him as he scanned the surrounding area, searching for any clue. Had someone else discovered the secret of Dwarka's depths and taken the ancient weapon? With a heavy heart, he swam back to the surface, the weight of his failure pressing down on him.

"Who are you, Son? I have not seen anyone dive into the deep waters for so long holding their breath.". The old man felt a wave of relief as he saw Ashwatthama return. He had been deeply worried, fearing that the mighty ocean might have claimed him forever.

"No Sir, I didn't hold my breath. I had this small oxygen cylinder with me" He had come prepared to make his story believable, ensuring his true identity was hidden.

"Shall we go back?" The old man asked him.

"Yes"

"Did you find what you were looking for?"

"No. Was there any activity done in this region?". Ashwatthama was curious to know.

"Yes, some government officials did some search, but it was 500 meters to the north"

They arrived at the shore before sunrise. Ashwatthama assured the fisherman that he would begin the repairs that very day. However, his mind was preoccupied—he needed to uncover what had happened to his mace.

"It has been stolen. But I will not rest until I retrieve it."

The promise hung in the air, as heavy as the ancient ruins submerged beneath the sea.

"Someone has leaked the secret or found some information about it. This cannot be a coincidence that three of our elements are missing" Sage Vyasa shared his concern with Ashwatthama over the Ghan.

The sun began its ascent, casting a golden hue across the sacred waters of the Ganges. The ghats of Varanasi, ancient and revered, buzzed with early morning activity. Amidst the chants of pilgrims and the rhythmic splashes of bathers, Adityadev sat cross-legged on a well-worn mat at Dashashwamedh Ghat, the most famous of them all.

Adityadev, in his early forties, exuded an aura of vibrant energy. His saffron robes fluttered lightly in the morning breeze, and a red tilak adorned his forehead, signifying his devotion and priestly duties. A small canopy shielded him from the sun, and around him, an array of puja items were meticulously arranged: brass lamps, incense sticks, conch shells, marigold garlands, and silver bowls filled with holy water and vermilion.

His eyes, sharp yet serene, scanned the throng of devotees and tourists. He greeted familiar faces with a nod and a gentle smile, his hands occasionally raising to bless someone in the crowd. The scent of burning camphor and sandalwood wafted through the air, mingling with the earthy smell of the river.

A family approached, their hands folded in respect. The father, dressed in a simple kurta-pajama, spoke, "Pandit ji, we wish to perform a Ganga Aarti and offer prayers for our ancestors."

Adityadev's face lit up with a welcoming smile. "Of course. Please, sit. We shall begin shortly."

As the family settled down, Adityadev began the preparations with practiced ease. His hands moved gracefully, lighting the lamps, arranging the flowers, and reciting sacred mantras with a melodic cadence that resonated with the divine ambiance of the ghat. The river's gentle flow mirrored the serenity of his chant, creating a harmonious backdrop. The ritual proceeded, drawing the attention of passersby who paused to witness the spiritual ceremony. As the family offered their prayers and floated a Diya on the Ganges, Adityadev's voice rose in a final invocation, blessing them with peace and prosperity.

Sage Vyasa was in a profession that was not alien to him. As Adityadev, he felt very normal where he didn't need to change a lot to mingle with the crowd. The last evening, he had visited the Ratneshwar Mahadev temple, which was surrounded by the sacred Ganges, adding to the mystical allure of the place. It was renowned for its dramatic tilt of about nine degrees, amplifying the significance of number nine in Hindu mythology.

The number nine holds profound significance, symbolizing completeness and eternity. It represents the nine forms of the Goddess Durga, the nine planets (Navagraha), and is associated with spiritual enlightenment and cosmic order.

Last morning, as the first light of dawn began to paint the sky with hues of gold and orange, Adityadev, the venerable priest, made his way through the cobbled streets of the town. He was a figure both respected and revered, his wisdom sought by many. Adityadev approached a modest but well-kept house, adorned with colorful threads and fabrics hanging from the windows and porch. The head of the Varma family, Raghav Varma, a man of quiet dignity and skilled hands, was already at work, his loom clacking rhythmically as he wove yet another masterpiece.

"Namaste, Raghav ji," Adityadev greeted with a slight bow, his voice carried the warmth of familiarity.

"Namaste, Pandit ji," Raghav replied and rose from his seat. "How can I serve you today?"

Adityadev looked around, ensuring their conversation remained private. "I come with a special request," he said softly, leaning in. "I need the Vayajanti Malla."

Raghav's eyes widened slightly at the mention of the secret code, understanding the gravity and sanctity of the request. The Vayajanti Malla was not a flag nor was it a piece of garment; it was an auspicious item left in the possession and guardship of the family which carried a deep spiritual significance.

"Of course, Pandit ji," Raghav responded, his voice filled with reverence. "I was told by my father that one day a revered sage will come to our doorsteps and ask for his possession. I am honored and blessed to be at your service"

Adityadev nodded appreciatively. "The temple relies on your family's dedication, Raghav ji. Your craftsmanship brings not just beauty but blessings to our shrine."

After a while, Adityadev and Raghav Varma stood at the edge of Manikarnika Ghat, the atmosphere filled with the scent of incense and the murmur of morning prayers. Before them loomed the ancient Ratneshwar Mahadev Temple, its spire piercing the sky, while its base remained partially submerged in the timeless waters of the Ganges.

Raghav glanced at Adityadev, who gave a solemn nod. Without hesitation, Raghav stepped into the cold, sacred river, his movements fluid and purposeful. The water embraced him, swirling around as if acknowledging his reverence. He took a deep breath and dove beneath the surface, disappearing into the murky depths.

Adityadev watched intently, chanting prayers under his breath. Moments felt like hours as he waited, the anticipation palpable. Raghav emerged after a few seconds, water cascading off him like a shimmering veil. In his hand, he held a cylindrical stone, its surface slick and glistening in the morning light.

"Pandit ji," Raghav called, wading back to the shore. "I have it."

Adityadev stepped forward, his eyes widening with awe as he took the stone from Raghav's hands. "This is it," he whispered, recognizing the sacred Shivalinga, a symbol of divine energy and cosmic creation.

"You've done well, Raghav ji," Adityadev said, his voice filled with gratitude. With folded hands, Adityadev bowed down to Raghav for his services and parted ways with him.

Adityadev walked back to his humble abode, the weight of the cylindrical stone in his bag was a reminder of the sacred mission. The streets of Varanasi buzzed with life, but his mind was focused on the task at hand. Reaching his modest home, he entered the dimly lit room filled with the fragrance of sandalwood and incense.

With careful hands, Adityadev took the stone out of his bag and placed it on a wooden table. He examined it closely, his fingers tracing the intricate carvings that adorned its surface. Taking a deep breath, he began to twist one end of the stone, just as one might open the cap of a bottle. The stone resisted at first, but with a little persistence, it yielded, revealing its secret.

The stone opened up to reveal a hollow chamber within. Tucked inside was a small necklace, its delicate chain adorned with shimmering blue stones that glinted in the dim light. Adityadev's eyes widened in awe as he carefully lifted the necklace, the weight of its significance dawning on him.

"This is no ordinary ornament," he murmured to himself, recognizing the rare Vayajanti Malla, a sacred but cursed necklace.

He gently placed the necklace back into the hollow chamber and closed the stone with the same reverence he had opened it.

Kumara, a dedicated cook in the bustling town of Trincomalee, set out early one morning on a mission that had consumed his thoughts since his arrival. Clutched tightly in his hand was a unique artifact, a small intricately carved wooden emblem, which served as a sign of a significant agreement. His destination was a banana farm owned by Mahesh, a well-respected farmer known throughout the region for his exceptional produce.

The sun was just beginning to rise, casting a golden hue over the verdant fields, as Kumara arrived at Mahesh's farm. The air was filled with the scent of ripe bananas, mingling with the earthy aroma of the soil. Mahesh was already hard at work, inspecting his crops with a critical eye when he noticed Kumara approaching. He straightened up, wiping the sweat from his brow, and greeted the cook with a warm smile.

"Kumara, it's good to see you. What brings you here so early?" Mahesh asked, his curiosity piqued by the rare sight of Kumara away from his kitchen.

Without a word, Kumara reached into his satchel and pulled out the wooden emblem. The artifact was small, fitting comfortably in the palm of his hand, but its significance was immense. The emblem was intricately carved with ornate designs and sacred Hindu symbols, such as lotus motifs and swirls of divine scripts, embodying cosmic harmony and signifying an ancient, unbroken pact forged by their forebears in reverence to dharma.

Mahesh's eyes widened in recognition. "This... this is the artifact of our forefathers," he whispered, his voice tinged with awe. "I thought it was lost forever."

Kumara nodded. "I found it hidden among my grandmother's belongings after she passed away. She always spoke of the bond our families shared, sealed by this very artifact. I believe it's time to honor that bond once more."

Mahesh stood silent for a moment, absorbing the weight of Kumara's words. Then, with a determined look, he motioned for Kumara to follow him. They walked towards Mahesh's modest home, located at the edge of the banana grove. Once inside, Mahesh rummaged through an old chest, retrieving a sturdy hammer with a wooden handle.

"This hammer," Mahesh explained, "is used in a ritual that our ancestors performed to honor their agreements. It symbolizes strength and commitment."

With the hammer in hand, Mahesh led Kumara through a winding path that eventually opened up to a magnificent view of the Koneswaram temple. The ancient temple stood majestically on a rocky promontory, overlooking the vast expanse of the Indian Ocean. Its stone walls were adorned with intricate carvings and statues, testaments to the rich history and culture of their people.

As they ascended the temple steps, they could hear the soft murmur of prayers. Mahesh and Kumara approached the temple's inner sanctum, where a large, flat stone lay at the center. This stone, Mahesh explained, was the sacred spot where their ancestors had made their vows. There was a carving of the Serpents "Nagas" above the rock, which was very intimidating. Kneeling beside a stone, Mahesh placed the wooden emblem in the center which fitted perfectly on the carvings. He started to tap slowly on the wooden emblem, on each tap a small compartment formed in the bottom of the Naga statue.

Kumara inserted his hand into the compartment. He found a white rock similar to a marble, with a carving of a serpent. The serpent was the representation of all the great snakes that belonged to the Naga family. He grabbed the artifact.

CHAPTER FIVE

THE STEAL

Satyaprakash had died and Arvind had completed his studies. He had started to become obsessive about deciphering the secrets in the notepad and The Scroll that his grandfather had given to him. He was trying to find connections with the various events and stories in Hindu scriptures and had traveled to many places in search of knowledge. He wanted to unravel the secrets that had been lost with time. He didn't know where this would take him, but the words from his Grandfather had stayed with him. Immortality felt a very far-fetched thought, but he knew if he dedicated some time and effort, he could discover something meaningful that would give him solace.

During his studies and exploration, he got to know about Professor Rao. He learned about his vast knowledge of the scriptures, theology, and archeology. The thought of discussing this with such a learned person in this field always excited Arvind. In pursuit of contact with the Professor, Arvind called the University where the Professor used to teach and give lectures. On persistent request, the University's admin gave up on the secrecy and shared the professor's phone number with Arvind. Arvind promised that he wouldn't disclose the source of this information to Professor.

One evening around seven, he called the Professor. He had kept his questions ready and was driven to leave a good first impression on the Professor. He did not fail.

"Hello Professor Rao Sir, I am Arvind Mishra speaking from Varanasi Sir" Arvind introduced himself in a confident yet submissive tone.

"Yes, speaking. What can I do for you?" Professor responded in a stern voice.

"I am a student of Hindu scriptures and symbols. My family has been in this profession for generations. We also collect ancient scriptures and artifacts to preserve and sell to museums and collectors."

"I don't intend to buy or sell anything, thank you"

"Sir, I don't intend to sell anything. I wanted to discuss with you an old scroll which I got from my Grandfather. He got it from his father and his father got it from his."

"What do you want from me? Come to the point. Who gave you my number?"

"Sir, I have been trying to contact you for weeks and have been calling your university. I got your number from them." Arvind broke his promise without even contemplating it. He was going to break another promise too, which he had given to his Grandfather, to share the secret preserved by his forefathers.

"Ok, what do you need?"

"I have artifacts, which my forefathers have been holding on to themselves as a secret. My grandfather believes that these can lead to supernatural powers, advanced technology, and even immortality."

"Immortality!!! No sane and knowledgeable person will speak like this, son. Study hard and grow in your business. All these ancient riddles and artifacts lead to dead ends, I have seen my share of these things. Don't waste your time."

"Sir, I just need a few hours of your time to show you what I have and what I think they lead to. If you feel they are rubbish, I will not bother you again. I'm curious sir, please don't decline."

"Where are you? You said you are in Varanasi."

"Sir, I will travel and come to you. You please give me a date"

Arvind was able to convince the Professor for a meeting. The professor gave his address and asked Arvind to drop by his house the following weekend. Arvind was excited and pleased to get this opportunity. He booked his train tickets and prepared for a long journey to the eastern coast of India, Berhampur. He took all his findings, the notebook, the scroll, and anything he found to be useful to convey his research and findings.

He arrived on a Saturday afternoon at Berhampur and took a cycle rickshaw from the railway station to Professor Rao's home. He knocked on the door. Professor Rao received him with a surprise as he didn't expect him to travel a couple of thousand kilometers just to meet and share his findings. He was impressed by Arvind's passion and dedication towards this. He welcomed him into the house and insisted he freshen up before getting into a discussion. Arvind arrived with a handbag and a suitcase. To the surprise of the Professor, Arvind opened the large suitcase to show the papers, scriptures, and images.

Professor Rao was engrossed with all the stories, tales, and findings of Arvind. He didn't utter a word for the first hour and consumed all the information that Arvind shared. Arvind emptied his mind, he didn't hesitate to share every information he had gathered. He was convinced that to tread further in this journey to unravel secrets he needed partners, professionals, and people with different perspectives. He had been looking at his information with the same lens and that had not helped him. Professor Rao went into a trance and was amazed at the possibilities of all this information. After a couple of hours of discussion and brainstorming, the Professor suggested a break. He prepared some filtered coffee, and although Arvind comes from the land of tea consumers, he happily gave company to the Professor. They went to the terrace to get some fresh air and clear their minds.

"I am amazed by all these, Arvind. Few of these stories I had heard and documented too, but the way you have connected the dots is incredible."

"So, you feel that there is a possibility that these can be true."

"I won't say 100% true, I would say that it is not 100% a myth. There have been so many scientific explanations for a lot of our scriptures and so-called mythological events. Some of the possible secrets like Nine Treasures of Kubera, the existence of Chintamani, Alchemy secrets, or the Amrit Kalash for immortality. They all have so many connections to earth and India. Where do we start?" Professor Rao responded in an optimistic tone.

"My Grandfather was certain about the Amrit Kalash. When he gave me The Scroll, he had told me that it is one of the seven keys to find it, although I think it is not the object but it is the information where the seven elements might be hidden. I think that would be a good starting point. If we find it, we will have enough time to spend in deciphering others." Arvind quipped.

"You are very greedy, Son. Who looks for treasures beyond immortality?

They both shared a laugh about the possibility of gaining access to an object that could give them immortality. For mere mortals, there can't be a greater high than this.

Over the next few months, they started to converse frequently over the phone to share and brainstorm on their theories. After a couple of years, the excitement to unveil the mysteries slowly died and they started to spend less time working on them. The daily brainstorming calls, which would go up to an hour-long discussion, had now become a weekly social pleasantries call to maintain the relationship. They traveled together a few times in the last two years to visit some temples where they spoke to the priests and administration departments and gained access to some ancient items, attended a couple of archeological summits, and browsed through a few of the libraries to accumulate knowledge. With fewer leads and success, the motivation was curbed down.

Professor Rao decided to go for the Chatur Dham trip across India. He started from Dwarka, on the west coast, then visited the Badrinath, in the north, where he fell ill and had to stop the journey. He returned to Berhampur, where he took a few days off to get back to good health. He decided to take blessings from the Lord Jagannath of Puri and then complete his pilgrimage at Rameswaram. The night before he headed to Puri, Arvind called Professor Rao to check on his health.

"Hello Sir, how are you feeling now?"

"Hello Arvind, I am doing well son. It was just a bit of exhaustion, so I decided to take a break for a few days."

"Yes, that is the wise thing to do. I am happy to hear that you are feeling better now."

"Thank you. How are you doing? Anything interesting since we last talked?"

"As you are going to travel to the Rameswaram temple, I was hoping you could meet someone in the temple, a priest or administration. We have not yet visited that particular temple and checked, we can get some information."

"Yes, sure. It is worth a try. I will take some of the artifacts and try enquiring there. I will be staying there for a couple of days, so will have some time in hand."

"Oh, great. So then take care of yourself. Have a good journey and we will speak once you are back"

"Thank you, you take care too"

During his visit to the Lord Jagannath temple, he met Gautam Mehta, a man in his late forties who was a small gem merchant in Surat. They connected quickly and explored the multiple tourist destinations of Puri together. They decided to give each other company while they traveled to their last destination to complete their pilgrimage journey. They took a train from Bhubaneswar to reach Rameswaram.

The train journey to Rameswaram over the Pamban Bridge was breathtaking. As the train chugged along, the vast expanse of the Indian Ocean unfolded on both sides, the turquoise water glistened under the sun. Excited to complete their holy pilgrimage, they both took the blessing of Lord Shiva in the temple, circled the place, and bathed in the 22 holy wells of the temple. They were left mesmerized by the sheer beauty and grandeur of the temple. Rao enquired around to get some time with some priests who had knowledge and understanding of the Hindu scriptures and their relevance to this place. They met Raghavan.

After the two days of stay at Rameswaram, Gautam and Professor Rao parted their ways to their respective destinations. Professor Rao took the train back and got down at the Berhampur railway station. He was feeling a sense of profound satisfaction in completing his endeavor. After freshening up, he had to give an update to Arvind who was waiting for his call.

"Hello Arvind, how are you? I just returned today from Rameswaram."

"Hello Sir, I am good. How was the trip?"

"It was great. The temple, the place, the people, and the food all were majestic."

"Wow, I am glad to hear it."

"Listen, I spoke to one of the priests. His name is Raghavan. He too acknowledged the Samudra Manthan episode where the Amrit drops had fallen on earth. Interestingly, he said in one of the many stories it is mentioned that they are protected by the Seven Chiranjeevis. They have taken the responsibility to protect this secret."

"Oh ok. That is not a far-fetched thought. Did he say anything about the location or the items?"

"Yes. He mentioned that they are hidden, both the seven Chiranjeevis and the items. If we can identify anyone, the other will be easier to discover. Some stories say that the items can be some of the symbols associated with Lord Vishnu like the Shankha (Conch Shell), Chakra (Disc), Gada (Mace), Padma (Lotus), Kastubha mani (Gem), Ananta (Serpent), Vaijayanti mala (Garland) and Srivatsa (Endless Circle mark)."

"What are your thoughts on this, sir?"

"We need to believe something and seek something, but we can never discard anything," Rao responded.

"Right. Let me see if I can find any mentions of these symbols, related to immortality"

"Sure, Arvind. I will do my bit, let us talk in a couple of days."

Arvind cross-referenced these symbols to his notes, scripts, and scroll. To his amazement, he found that few of these symbols of Lord Vishnu were mentioned in the scroll. He and Professor Rao continued their research and exploration with a newfound energy after the visit from Rameswaram. For the next few months, they again started their daily brainstorming sessions over the phone.

As time went on, their energy began to fade once more as the demands of life caught up with them. Arvind got married. Professor Rao visited Varanasi to bless the couple. Arvind had started to take full responsibility for taking care of his family and business. His uncle, Disnesh's health had started to spiral down while Arvind recalled his Grandfather's words about his family's curse. While he was taking care of his family's and society's responsibilities, whenever he got some time, he went back to the notebook shared by his Grandfather and looked at his notes. Rekha, his wife, also supported him in this passion and didn't mind the faded obsession. Professor Rao maintained his friendship with Arvind. They discussed family, finances, and politics in their weekly calls over the phone.

Pallavi, a vibrant young woman in her late 20s, was buzzing with excitement as she prepared for a significant day—her marriage shopping in Thiruvananthapuram. With her trusted friend Kalpana by her side, the day promised to be both productive and delightful. Thiruvananthapuram, with its rich cultural heritage and vibrant markets, was the perfect destination for their shopping spree.

Their primary destination was Shanti Boutique, a place that had recently become the talk of the town. Renowned for its exquisite collection and impeccable service, Shanti Boutique had received rave reviews from friends and family. This boutique, known for its unique blend of traditional and contemporary designs, was highly recommended for brides-to-be.

Pallavi and Kalpana were particularly excited to explore the boutique's extensive range of sarees and dresses, perfect for the myriad rituals and ceremonies that await. From the engagement to the wedding day, and the reception to post-wedding gatherings, each event required a unique outfit. They had heard that Shanti Boutique offered a wide variety of options, from luxurious silk sarees adorned with intricate zari work to elegant lehengas and chic designer dresses.

As they walked into the boutique, the welcoming ambiance and the sight of beautiful fabrics and stunning ensembles instantly captivated them. The friendly staff greeted them warmly, ready to assist in selecting the perfect attire for Pallavi's special day. Amara came up to Pallavi and enquired about her needs and expectations, promising to cater to each one of them. Amara had returned from Indore last evening after cementing some deals with textile and handloom wholesalers. This was her second visit in the last couple of months. She wanted to expand her collection and cater to all the fashion needs in the town.

"When do you have your ring ceremony? And what are you planning to wear? Amara inquired.

"I have planned to wear sarees in all occasions except the feast reception, where I plan to wear lehenga" Pallavi responded with a tinge of excitement.

"What do you think? Will that be a good idea?" Kalpana asked Amara

"Yes, that will be perfect. Take a look at the collection, we have many designs and colors for you. Take your time and call me if you need anything."

"Thank you, Amara"

Amara got back to her pod placed near the entrance where she kept an eye on the proceedings from a monitor integrated with CCTV cameras. She had a small shelf where she kept her accounting and billing books.

There was not much of a crowd in the shop, Pallavi could demand all the attention in the shop. Amara ordered some filter coffees from the nearby stall. She was impressed by the knowledge and understanding of fashion that Pallavi possessed, while Pallavi was equally impressed with the collection in front of her. She was overwhelmed with choices and was not able to pick any. Amara dived in to help.

"Think of what kind of makeup you would put on for each occasion, and what type of ritual will it be. Consider comfort too while choosing, because you will need to wear them for most hours in a day"

Pallavi appreciated the advice and was finally able to make up her mind.

The items were invoiced and a good healthy discount was also offered to the to-be bride as a wedding gift from the boutique. This was a smart marketing trick which had made Amara's business flourish in such a cluttered and competitive space. Amara knew how to build relations and keep her customers happy.

Pallavi, before leaving, invited Amara to her engagement and wedding ceremonies. Amara accepted the offer with humility and promised her presence. She thought this could potentially be a great event to garner more customers and connections.

After a couple of days, one evening while Amara was lying on her bed and enjoying some melodious Malayalam songs, she got a call.

"Hi Amara, this is Rakesh here. I had called you at noon, but realized that you would have gone to your boutique. I don't have your boutique's number."

"Hi, Rakesh. Oh yes, I left for the boutique at 8 AM today. As I was away for a few days, I had to check the accounts and stocks before opening. Tell me, what happened?"

"I wanted to thank you. Ravi can stand up now. I think he is getting stronger. I know I was not very welcoming to your idea of using pooja, mantras, and rituals to cure anything. I hope you understand that." Rakesh confided with Amara.

"Don't worry Ravi. I am happy that Ravi is getting better."

"All my life I have read and understood that science is everything. I was never very religious or superstitious. So, when you said that you have been studying and practicing poojas and mantras, which I still don't understand, it was very difficult for me to accept. If Anjali had not been there, I might have never gone with the rituals. But now that I am seeing this, I am glad that we did it."

"When did you start seeing some improvement with Ravi?"

"A few days, maybe a week after you left, Ravi started to feel stronger. Yesterday, he again stood up without any support. I wanted, I mean we wanted to know, is there anything else we can do to improve his health further"

"These are occult science and dark powers, Rakesh. I know these powers and their capability. We should use it only when needed. I can understand your feeling as a parent, but there is a price we all need to pay if we get something."

"I didn't get you, Amara. Is it about money?"

"No, Rakesh. The price is life and death. The most precious thing we mortal beings possess is life. The dark powers are always hungry for more power."

"I am not getting you, Amara. Can you please lay it out for me? We are ready to go to any limits to save our son."

"There are some things which I am also not aware. I will let you know once I come to know"

"Ok, fine. But thank you again. We owe everything to you. One more thing, Amara. Please do not refuse. In two months, it is Ravi's sixth birthday. We would be very happy if you could come. Please don't refuse. You don't have to worry a bit, I will make all the arrangements. You just pack your bags and come. Please ...."

"Of course, how can I miss Ravi's birthday?"

"I hope he feels better during his birthday." Rakesh sounded a bit concerned.

"Don't worry. He will feel better."

"Goodbye, Amara."

They both hung up the phone. Amara sat in thought, searching for ways to appease the dark forces and ensure they continued to bless Ravi. Over time, she had learned to communicate with the dead and understand the demands of these shadowy entities. To keep Ravi safe—and perhaps even find a cure—she would need to perform a series of rituals.

"But at what cost?" she wondered as she prepared for bed. She was well aware that every revelation that reached her was also being whispered into the ears of the dark forces.

After a few days, Amara attended Pallavi's ring ceremony where she met her family and the great sculptor artist, Anandan, Pallavi's father. She was welcomed to the ceremony and treated like a family member. She thoroughly enjoyed the evening and started to make a bond with Pallavi. Pallavi also looked at her like an elder sister, and role model, and started to adore her company. Amara's independence, charm, and strong personality had a lasting effect on all the ladies in the ceremony. Pallavi frequently visited the boutique to spend time with Amara. She ran all her fashion through her and followed her advice religiously. Amara reciprocated by getting some modern and fashionable accessories for her and started to visit her house frequently.

During the marriage ceremony, Pallavi didn't leave Amara out of her sight and wanted her by her side through all the rituals. It was like Amara had put a spell on Pallavi, but this had nothing to do with the occult science or dark forces. It was coming from a space of true admiration and love. Pallavi got married and a beautiful ceremony ended with joy and tears. Amara was back to her business.

Amara attended Ravi's vibrant 6th birthday party, a cheerful event filled with colorful balloons, lively music, and the laughter of children. True to his word, Rakesh had taken care of all travel arrangements, allowing Amara to arrive at the celebration without any hassle. As she stepped into the festively decorated venue, Amara was greeted by the sight of Ravi, beaming with joy, surrounded by his friends, all eagerly diving into games and activities.

Amara moved through the crowd, enjoying the festive atmosphere. She soon found herself in a pleasant conversation with Arvind, who she learned was Rakesh's brother-in-law. Arvind had a friendly demeanor, with an easy smile that suggested he was no stranger to fun. They exchanged stories about Ravi's antics and shared laughter over amusing family anecdotes.

"Here is your gift, my hero"

Amara pulled out a gold chain with a pendant shaped like a Mandala.

> "*In Hinduism, a mandala is an intricate, circular design symbolizing the universe and its divine order. These geometric patterns represent cosmic harmony and balance, used as spiritual tools in rituals, meditation, and temple art. Mandalas often contain squares, circles, and lotus motifs, each with deep symbolic meanings related to spiritual concepts and deities. They serve as visual aids to focus the mind during meditation, aiding in spiritual growth and self-realization. The creation and contemplation of mandalas are considered sacred practices, fostering a connection between the individual and the divine, reflecting the unity and order of the cosmos.*"

"Thank you, Amara Aunty." Ravi received it with a smile.

"This was unnecessary, Amara." Anjali reacted when she saw that it was a gold chain.

"It is not for you, Anjali. It is for my hero. This will keep him strong"

Rakesh and Anjali had swells in their eyes. They understood what it meant and what it meant to Ravi's life. They both hugged Amara.

Rakesh took Amara to one corner of the room.

"Is this it? Will it cure it?"

"No, no Rakesh. I have not yet reached there. The forces are giving me some symbols which I am not able to decipher. They tend to play with riddles and puzzles. It is not easy, Rakesh. I may never be able to crack it. So please don't have high hopes, I will do whatever I can"

"You know what. Arvind can help us. He has been studying scriptures, symbols, and whatnot from a very young age. He is family. He is Anjali's elder brother."

"Have you told him about my .. ?" Amara was tensed.

"He doesn't know the details. He knows that you are a practitioner of mantras and tantras. He knows you are gifted. He has traveled from Varanasi to meet you."

"Oh ok. Rakesh, please keep these things a secret. You never know how it will affect Ravi"

"Yes, sure. Don't worry. I just want to help."

"Ok. I will speak with Arvind."

Amara started to keep in touch with Arvind after this event. Amara would discuss with Arvind the various signs or signals she would get from her interactions with the dark forces. She remained secretive about the various acts she had indulged in, to be ageless or protect her friend's son from a fatal disease, but simultaneously she used all the knowledge Arvind possessed on symbols and scriptures to solve her riddles. They discussed the various aspects of life and their relevance in the scriptures. Over the next few years, they both exchanged notes over the phone and met a couple of times at social events hosted by Rakesh and his family. Arvind had started to confide with Amara.

It had been a few years since Prof. Rao had met with Raghavan. Arvind had also paid a few visits to Rameswaram to meet him and had gained acquaintance with him as well.

Raghavan walked along the narrow, winding streets of Rameswaram, his saffron robes billowing slightly in the sea breeze. The sun had just begun to set, casting an orange glow over the ancient town. The air was thick with the mingled scents of saltwater and incense, a reminder of the countless prayers that had risen from this place. His sandals slapped against the cobblestones as he made his way toward the marketplace, where he knew Daru would be wrapping up his day.

Daru, a humble vendor, sold trinkets and religious paraphernalia to the throngs of pilgrims who visited the famous Rameswaram temple. Despite his modest occupation, Daru was the son of the Chief Priest Ramanatha, a man whose name carried weight within the temple walls. Raghavan had heard whispers of a hidden treasure, secrets religiously guarded by the chief priests over generations. If the rumors held any truth, Daru might possess knowledge that could lead Raghavan to this treasure. But to access this information, he first needed to gain Daru's trust.

As Raghavan approached the bustling marketplace, he spotted Daru's stall, adorned with brightly colored beads, small statues, and other religious artifacts. Daru, a man in his early thirties with a lean frame and a friendly demeanor, was closing up for the day. Raghavan put on a warm smile and walked over.

"Namaste, Daru," he greeted, his voice carrying the practiced warmth of a seasoned priest. "It seems the gods have blessed you with a busy day."

Daru looked up, momentarily surprised, but then his face broke into a welcoming smile. "Namaste, Raghavan. Yes, the temple has been crowded with pilgrims today. It's been a good day."

Raghavan nodded, glancing around at the dispersing crowd. "Would you care to join me for some coffee? It's been a long day for both of us, I'm sure."

Daru hesitated for a moment, then nodded. "Of course. There's a coffee stall nearby. Let's go."

The two men walked together to the small, unassuming coffee stall at the edge of the market. They settled onto a pair of wooden stools, and soon, steaming cups of coffee were placed before them. Raghavan sipped his coffee, savoring the spicy warmth, while he studied Daru from the corner of his eye.

"You know, Daru," Raghavan began, "I've always admired your dedication. Running a stall like yours, amidst the ebb and flow of pilgrims, must be a challenge."

Daru shrugged modestly. "It's a simple life, but it's honest work. I'm content."

Raghavan smiled, nodding thoughtfully. "Contentment is a rare treasure. Your father, Ramanatha, is a revered man. His wisdom and guidance shaped this temple in so many ways."

A shadow flickered across Daru's face at the mention of his father. "Yes, he is a great man. I respect and adore him."

Raghavan reached out, placing a comforting hand on Daru's shoulder. "His legacy will live on through you, Daru. I was wondering if he ever shared with you any of the temple's deeper secrets, its hidden history?"

Daru looked at Raghavan, a hint of suspicion in his eyes. "Why do you ask, Raghavan?"

Raghavan leaned back, adopting an air of casual curiosity. "I've been delving into the temple's history myself. There are so many layers to it, so many stories yet untold. I thought perhaps you might have some insights, something that could help me understand our heritage better."

Daru took a long sip of his coffee, his gaze never leaving Raghavan's face. "My father did share stories with me, but they were personal, meant for family. The temple's history is vast, but some things are best left undisturbed."

Raghavan's heart sank slightly. Daru was more guarded than he had anticipated. He needed to tread carefully. "Of course, Daru. I respect that. I didn't mean to intrude. I just believe that understanding our past can help us honor it more deeply."

Daru relaxed a little, his expression softening. "I understand. My father did speak of hidden things, but they were shrouded in allegory and parables. Even I don't know what's true and what's myth."

Raghavan nodded, his mind racing. Allegories and parables could be deciphered with the right knowledge. He decided to change the subject, letting the conversation flow more naturally, and building a genuine rapport. They talked about their daily lives, the people of Rameswaram, and the countless pilgrims who passed through the town.

As the evening wore on, Raghavan felt a growing sense of camaraderie with Daru. He realized that this friendship would not be an easy means to an end. Daru was a man of integrity, and earning his trust would require genuine effort. As they parted ways, Raghavan knew he had taken the first step, but the path ahead was long and uncertain. He resolved to walk it with patience and sincerity, hoping that in time, Daru would share the secrets he sought.

Over the next few months, Raghavan and Daru's friendship deepened. Raghavan's persistent kindness and genuine interest in Daru's life had created a bond of trust between them. They met frequently, discussing everything from temple affairs to the nuances of their personal lives. Raghavan was patient, never pushing too hard for information but always subtly steering conversations toward the temple's mysteries.

One monsoon evening, as the rain hammered against the rooftops, Raghavan and Daru sat in Daru's modest home, warmed by the glow of an oil lamp. The storm had cut the power, and the rhythmic drumming of the rain created a cocoon of intimacy around them. They were sipping hot coffee, reminiscing about their shared experiences.

"Raghavan," Daru began, his voice contemplative, "do you remember when you first asked me about the temple's secrets?"

Raghavan looked up, surprised by the sudden shift in conversation. "Of course, Daru. But I stopped pressing you on that long ago. I respect your privacy."

Daru nodded, a small smile playing on his lips. "You've been a true friend, Raghavan. And I've come to trust you completely. My father once told me that true friendship is the only treasure worth seeking. I believe he was right."

Raghavan felt a flutter of hope in his chest. He chose his words carefully. "Your father is a wise man. I'm honored by your trust, Daru."

Daru took a deep breath, his eyes reflecting the flickering lamp light. "There is something I've been hesitant to share, but I feel it's time. My father did tell me about the temple's hidden treasures. He said they were not just material wealth but spiritual artifacts, meant to protect and guide the temple's future, and only our family is entrusted with this task of guarding this secret"

Raghavan listened intently, his heart pounding. Daru continued, his voice steady. "Beneath the temple, there's a concealed chamber. It's accessible only through a hidden passage behind the sanctum. My father showed it to me once, swearing me to secrecy. Inside, there are ancient texts, precious stones, and relics believed to possess divine powers."

Raghavan's mind raced with the possibilities. "Why did your father keep this secret, Daru?"

"He believed that revealing it would disrupt the temple's sanctity and attract those who sought power and wealth over spiritual enlightenment. He wanted to ensure that only those truly worthy would ever find it."

Raghavan nodded, understanding the gravity of the knowledge he had just been entrusted with. "Thank you for sharing this with me, Daru. I promise to honor your father's wishes and protect this secret."

Daru smiled, relief was evident in his eyes. "I know you will, Raghavan. You've proven yourself a true friend. Together, we can ensure the temple's legacy remains pure and untainted."

As the storm raged outside, Raghavan felt a deep sense of fulfillment. His patience and sincerity had finally been rewarded, and he vowed to safeguard the treasure with the same devotion he had shown in cultivating his friendship with Daru.

Raghavan began his exploration with a newfound sense of purpose, guided by the fragments of information Daru provided. Each week, he would visit Daru, subtly steering their conversations toward the temple's hidden passages. Daru, slowly opening up, shared small but crucial details.

On one occasion, Daru mentioned a specific inscription on a pillar near the sanctum that hinted at a concealed doorway. Raghavan, under the guise of performing routine temple duties, examined the pillar closely. Hidden beneath layers of ancient script, he found a faint outline of a door. Encouraged, Raghavan returned to Daru, who then spoke of a particular prayer chant that, when recited, revealed the door's mechanism. Intrigued, Raghavan spent nights in the temple, chanting softly until he heard a faint click. A hidden panel slid open, revealing a narrow, dimly lit passage.

Over months, Daru's snippets of wisdom accumulated. He spoke of specific steps to avoid, warning of traps set to deter intruders. Raghavan navigated the labyrinthine corridors, each step a calculated risk based on Daru's careful guidance. One evening, Daru shared a vital piece of the puzzle: a map his father had drawn, showing the exact route through the maze-like passages. Raghavan copied the map meticulously, ensuring every detail was accurate. Armed with this, he ventured deeper than ever before.

Finally, after months of cautious exploration and piecing together Daru's knowledge, Raghavan reached a heavy stone door adorned with ancient carvings. He chanted the prayer Daru had taught him and pushed. The door creaked open, revealing a chamber filled with treasures beyond imagination—gleaming jewels, ancient texts, and relics radiating a soft, ethereal glow.

Raghavan's heart pounded as he carefully retraced his steps through the hidden passage. In his hands, he clutched a small silver Shivling and a blue conch, relics he believed held spiritual significance. He had left the jewels and gold untouched, feeling their allure was unworthy compared to these sacred artifacts.

As he emerged from behind the sanctum, he froze. The stern face of one of the main priests loomed in the dim light. The priest's eyes narrowed, his gaze locking onto the items in Raghavan's hands. Raghavan had locked the secret gateway before he was caught by the priest.

"What are you doing here, Raghavan?"

Raghavan stammered, trying to explain. "I... I found these items hidden behind the main sanctum chamber. They need to be protected."

"You've violated the temple's sanctity. These items are not yours to take."

Raghavan ran towards the west gate, but before he could get away from the temple guards on duty, they were quick to get hold of him. Shortly after the police arrived, Raghavan hid the blue conch under a banyan tree. Raghavan was arrested, and the Shivalinga was confiscated and returned to the Chief priest. As he was led away in handcuffs, Raghavan's mind raced. He had been caught, and his fate lay in the hands of those who couldn't understand his true purpose.

After three long years in jail, Raghavan, a devoted priest, was finally released. The moment he stepped out, his mind was filled with a singular purpose: to seek the blessings of Lord Shiva at the revered Rameswaram temple. The journey to the temple was both a pilgrimage and a homecoming for Raghavan, who had served there faithfully before his imprisonment.

Upon reaching the temple, he felt a wave of peace and reverence wash over him. He entered the sanctum and prostrated himself before the deity, his heart heavy with remorse and hope. The familiar chants and the scent of incense enveloped him, and he prayed fervently, seeking forgiveness and divine guidance.

With his spiritual duty fulfilled, Raghavan made his way to the outer corridor of the temple. He walked with a sense of urgency and trepidation towards the old banyan tree that stood there, its roots sprawling across the ground. This tree held a secret that had burdened him for years. He knelt by the tree and began to dig carefully, his hands trembling. After a few moments, he uncovered the item he had stolen and hidden there long ago. As he held it, a mixture of relief and guilt surged through him. He walked back to his home and kept the Conch safely in a tin box where he had kept all the items that he had received from Professor Rao, and slid it under the kitchen shelf. He got the Professor's number from one of the papers inside the box and walked to the nearby phone booth.

"Professor Rao, I am Raghavan from Rameswaram." Raghavan was confident that Professor Rao would recognize him. The Professor had visited a couple of times more with Arvind to share more insights about their research and exploration.

"Namaste, Raghavan. I heard about what happened. I visited, but you were not there. How are you now?" Professor spoke in a soft voice showing sympathy.

"I am ok. I have got it."

"You found it. Was that the reason for your imprisonment?" The professor was surprised.

"Yes, I got caught but I have no regrets. I did it with my full consciousness. I know Lord Shiva will forgive me"

"Ok. Hold on to the item and keep it safe. Try to take a different profession and stay away as much as possible from the temple. If someone comes to know that you are in possession of such an item, you might get punished again."

"Yes, ok. I will open a small shop by the beach. I have thought of it"

"Ok good. Do you have any number? Can you take a mobile phone which can be only used for our discussion? Take a prepaid one, ok."

"Ok, I will get it today and give you the number."

"We have to maintain secrecy going forward, otherwise all of us will be implicated, Raghavan."

"I understand"

Professor Rao felt a rush in his adrenaline after hearing the news. He immediately dialed Arvind to give him the news.

After the initial pleasantries, Professor Rao spoke in a soft voice.

"Raghavan has got it, Arvind. We can follow our theory and try to find the remaining ones."

"Oh God. I don't know how to react, Professor, this is big!!!"

"Yes, but from now onwards we need to maintain a certain level of secrecy to this. Till now these were all stories that we could share and speak to each other, but with this item available and in our possession we need to be careful"

"I agree."

"Who else knows about our quest?" Professor asked with a concern in his voice.

"Not many. Rekha, Rakesh, Anjali and Amara know."

"Get Amara in confidence, others are family so need not worry"

"Yes, I will speak with her."

"Sir, you mentioned that when you first met with Raghavan there was another person with you as well in the discussion. Do you think he can be a threat?"

"Oh yes. I forgot about Gautam. I will speak with him."

Arvind had been contemplating the call for days, knowing it would change everything. When he finally dialed Amara's number, his heart pounded with a mix of fear and anticipation. Amara answered on the third ring, her voice warm and curious.

"Hey, Arvind! What's up?" she greeted cheerfully.

Arvind took a deep breath, his mind racing through the carefully guarded secrets he was about to unveil. "Amara, I need to tell you something important," he began, his voice trembling slightly. "There are things I've been wanting to tell you."

"Yes, Arvind. I am all ears."

"You know Professor Rao, with whom I do a lot of research on the ancient scriptures and symbols. We have been working together for over two decades."

"Yes, I know that. That is not a secret, Arvind."

"Yes. You don't know how it started"

For the next few minutes, Arvind shared about all the life events that had happened in their quest. He shared about his grandfather's notebook, which he got on his 16th birthday, the story about the Samudra Manthan and the events that happened after that, his visit to Professor Rao's home, the pilgrimage journey of Professor Rao, Raghavan's adventure, and Gautam. Amara was left speechless after hearing the whole story.

"Are you saying that there is a possibility of having Immortality if we have all the elements? And you are saying that you know where they would be present?"

"Far-fetched idea. But with Raghavan getting an artifact which might be one of them, we are hopeful that we could find the remaining in our lifetime."

"Oh right," Amara responded sarcastically.

"I know what you're thinking. But please, can you keep this information with you? As it involves Raghavan and his theft from the temple, we don't want any implications on us but would continue on the pursuit."

"Yes absolutely. Who else knows about it?"

"Now you, Rakesh, Anjali, Rekha, Raghavan, Gautam, and Professor Rao."

"Ok. A big group!!!"

"From now onwards, we have agreed to discuss this topic in secrecy. Can you get a separate phone for yourself, we can use that phone to contact you"?

"Ok, sure. I will get one. But are we going to get in trouble?"

"No, No. No one would believe in such things. We just want to be cautious."

"Ok."

The visit to the Chatur Dham had left a profound impression on Gautam. The knowledge shared during his discussions with Professor Rao lingered in his mind. The few days spent with the professor fostered a deep sense of respect and friendship between them. The myriad mysteries and stories he encountered during his visit sparked a lifelong curiosity within him. He continued to engage with the professor over the phone, often discussing topics such as life, spirituality, and legacy.

Gautam had always harbored a fear of God, a fear that intensified as he became more successful and wealthier. The anxiety of losing everything made him increasingly superstitious. He began consulting an astrologer for blessings and validation before making any business decisions. His visits to temples became more frequent, and he donated generously. Additionally, he wore various gems and stones to ward off bad luck.

"Hello Gautam, Professor Rao here" Professor called after knowing about Raghavan.

"Hello Professor, so nice to hear from" Gautam was surprised. It was not very often that Professor remembered Gautam.

"How are you, Gautam?"

"I am doing well. Is everything ok?"

"Yes, everything is ok. Do you have some time now? There was something I wanted to discuss with you and it needs your full attention."

"Yes, please tell."

"Gautam, I hope I can trust you with a deep secret that may sound insane. But you have to promise me that you will not utter a single word outside. It is a matter of life and death."

"You sound serious, Professor. You can rest assured that I am taking this secret to my last breath"

"Well, it is about that. If we succeed, it may never happen."

"What!! Death won't happen"

For the next few minutes, Professor Rao shared about Arvind, his ancestors, their visits to Rameswaram, Raghavan's deed, and the possibility of existence of the Elixir of life. He also shared about the people who know about this and why it is important to keep it a secret. It was too much for Gautam. He was dumbfounded.

"I need some time to think and process this, Professor. Are you serious?"

"Yes, I am. And I know this is a lot to process, take your time. But remember not to discuss it with anyone, not even your family. We cannot have any loose ends, we stop here."

Gautam had slowly started to process and started to deeply think about the possibility of becoming an immortal.He would spend hours on his terrace, wishfully thinking and imagining what he would do if he attained immortality. Out of curiousity, he once asked Arvind, "Will we get younger if we attain immortality or remain in the same age ?"

Arvind at first thought it to be a joke and laughed, but later sensed that Gautam had asked him with curiosity and seriousness.

"This is not the fountain of youth. This is immortality so I think we will stay the same age but just become immortal." Arvind responded.

The response hit Gautam differently. While being immortal was an exciting proposition, he would not live a happy immortal life with his current state of health. He became conscious of his health and started to follow a healthier diet and lifestyle.

"Hope does not change reality, but it changes people. And people, in turn, shape reality. In the end, hope is not just a feeling; it is the first step toward transformation."

Gautam first heard about the marine excavation in Dwarka from Arvind. Intrigued, Gautam began to delve deeper into the subject, spending hours reading articles and watching documentaries about the underwater excavation. The ancient city believed to be the legendary Dwarka of Lord Krishna, had always fascinated him, and now it seemed the myths were rooted in reality.

Driven by curiosity and the tantalizing possibility of uncovering secrets related to Vishnu, Gautam decided he needed to see the artifacts for himself. He made a trip to Dwarka, where the underwater excavation was still ongoing. The site was bustling with activity, with archaeologists and workers meticulously excavating and cataloging each find.

Gautam inquired about the findings, steering the conversation towards the symbols of Vishnu.

"The excavation had unearthed a plethora of ancient artifacts, including pottery, sculptures, and intricate carvings that speak of a long-lost civilization." One of the officials who was part of the excavation commented.

Among these artifacts were symbols associated with Vishnu, one of the principal deities in Hinduism. Gautam's interest was particularly piqued by the mention of one symbol—a small mace. This mace was not just a religious artifact but potentially a key to unlocking the immortality puzzle that had been the subject of his discussions with Professor Rao and Arvind.

As the conversation progressed, Gautam subtly hinted at his interest in acquiring the mace, suggesting it could be part of a private collection dedicated to preserving Indian heritage. The Officer, a man of principle, dismissed the idea, emphasizing the importance of keeping such artifacts in public museums for everyone to study and appreciate. Gautam realized that a different approach was needed. He discreetly inquired among the workers and lower-ranking corrupt officials, trying to find someone who might be more amenable to his proposition.

Eventually, he found an assistant, who was sympathetic to his cause and struggling with financial difficulties. Rajesh was initially hesitant, but Gautam's offer was too tempting to refuse. Gautam promised him a substantial sum of money in exchange for the small mace. They devised a plan where Rajesh would swap the mace with a replica during the cataloging process.

The real mace was handed over to Gautam, who carefully wrapped it and placed it in a secure briefcase. Rajesh received the money, and both parted ways, hoping their secret would remain undiscovered. Gautam felt a rush of exhilaration and guilt, knowing he had just acquired a significant piece of history through unethical means.

A few months had passed since Arvind revealed the secret to Amara. During this time, Amara had obtained a secret spare prepaid phone, which she kept hidden in her wooden almirah. All discussions about their quest were strictly conducted via these spare phones. Arvind and Rao had narrowed down their search to fifteen possible locations in India where they believed the elements could be found. After gaining insights from Raghavan, they concluded that these secrets might be guarded by certain families, such as the Chief Priest of Rameswaram or Arvind's own family. Arvind regretted not coming up with the idea of families guarding the secrets earlier, as it seemed so obvious in hindsight.

One of the secret locations was the Sree Padmanabhasway temple. Arvind and Professor shared their knowledge with Amara. They wanted her to speak with some of the local families in the town and gain knowledge about their legacy. Amara used her clientele and connections to speak with powerful families and tried to gather information about their family and ancestor's legacy. She did a lot of work and also used some influence of her dark forces. After a thorough investigation, she narrowed it down to a few families and one of them was Pallavi's.

Whenever Pallavi visited her home in Thiruvananthapuram, she made it a point to meet Amara. She would share every story and incident with Amara, seeking her validation. Amara would always smile and hug her, offering a sense of admiration that Pallavi could only find in her. Their friendship had deepened over the years.

It had been more than 15 years since they first met when Pallavi had visited Amara's boutique to buy sarees and dresses for her wedding. Amara had ensured that Pallavi received the best service as a customer. Pallavi received numerous compliments on her wedding attire from both her family and in-laws, and she credited Amara entirely for her excellent advice and service during the ceremony.

Pallavi had visited her home during the Alpsi festival. She had invited Amara for lunch and wanted to show her family's legacy, the sculpture and craft. Pallavi was very proud of her family's rich history and contribution to the famous relics of modern times. She had recently learned about the contribution of her family in the renovation of the Shree Padmanabhaswamy temple 500 years ago. She wanted to pay a visit to the temple before she left for her in-laws. Anandan, Pallavi's father made arrangements for her daughter and her friends to visit the temple.

Amara stepped through the towering gates of the Sree Padmanabhaswamy temple, flanked by her friends Pallavi and Kalpana. Pallavi's eyes sparkled with pride as she led them towards the first mandapam.

"This is the Kulasekhara Mandapam," Pallavi announced, her voice echoing softly in the sacred space. Amar marveled at the intricate carvings that adorned the pillars. Each figure seemed to tell a story, frozen in time by the skillful hands of Pallavi's ancestors.

Pallavi continued, "My family's craftsmen renovated these pillars. Look at the detailing on this one." She pointed to a pillar with delicate floral patterns interwoven with mythical creatures. Amara ran her fingers lightly over the carvings, feeling the grooves and ridges that brought the stone to life. They moved on to the next mandapam, the Dhwaja Mandapam, where Kalpana stopped to admire the ceiling. "This craftsmanship is incredible," she said, tilting her head back to take in the ornate patterns.

Pallavi smiled, "It took years of dedication and devotion. My grandfather often spoke of the labor and love poured into these works."

As they wandered through the temple, Amara felt a deep connection to the history and artistry around her, grateful to experience the legacy of Pallavi's family up close. The ancient temple seemed to whisper its secrets, each mandapam revealing stories of the past, beautifully preserved through generations.

Amara saw Anandan, Pallavi's father, standing near the Mukulakara Mandapam, his hands folded in reverent prayer. The serene expression on his face reflected his deep connection to the temple and its sacred surroundings. As Anandan finished his prayer, he glanced around, ensuring no one was watching. But Amara, curious and observant, noticed his movements from close quarters, hiding behind a large pillar.

Anandan moved towards one of the intricately carved pillars, his fingers deftly tracing the ancient designs. Amara watched intently as he pressed a specific sequence of carvings, almost like a ritual dance, unlocking a secret compartment that lay hidden within the stone. Her heart raced with excitement and anticipation as she committed each step to memory.

The compartment opened with a soft click. Anandan carefully glanced around once more before closing the compartment. Amara's mind buzzed with questions and curiosity about the box's contents and the compartment's purpose. After Anandan left, Amara seized the opportunity. She approached the same pillar, her fingers trembling slightly as she replicated the sequence she had seen. With a deep breath, she pressed the carvings in the exact order, and the secret compartment sprang open. Her excitement grew as she reached inside and pulled out the box, feeling the weight of its hidden significance.

She closed the compartment, ensuring it was securely locked before stepping back. The experience had deepened her appreciation for the temple and the dedication of Pallavi's family. With a newfound respect and curiosity, Amara rejoined her friends, carrying the weight of the secrets she had uncovered and the promise to safeguard them.

CHAPTER SIX

THE REVEAL

After calling all the members in the group, Arvind made his plans to travel to Dwarka. He planned to take a train from Varanasi to Indore, where he would pick his brother-in-law, and then headed towards his destination. The journey was long but comfortable, with occasional chats with fellow passengers and a few cups of tea bought from the vendors at various stops. Arvind had kept himself occupied by reading a novel and listening to music. After several hours, the train finally pulled into Indore Junction. Arvind stepped onto the platform, stretched his legs, and took a deep breath, eager to reunite with Rakesh.

Rakesh had arrived at the station to pick up Arvind and warmly welcomed him. They drove to Rakesh's house, where Arvind was shown to a cozy guest room. Grateful for the hospitality, Arvind rested for a few hours, recovering from the long train journey. Arvind and Rakesh had to travel to Dwarka the same evening. Rakesh had booked the tickets a couple of days prior and secured seats in comfortable AC compartments. They had dinner at home. Anjali had prepared delicious roti and rajma. After dinner, they hired a cab and headed to Indore station to catch their train to Dwarka. The cab ride was smooth with minimal traffic so they reached the station with plenty of time to spare. The anticipation of the journey ahead filled them with a sense of excitement and ease.

Amara had meticulously planned her journey from Thiruvananthapuram to Dwarka, ensuring every detail was in place.

She booked her train tickets, opting for a two-tier AC class to travel comfortably. Packing light, she included only essentials for the long journey and the anticipated changes in climate. Her train departed from Thiruvananthapuram Central Railway Station early in the morning. The journey was long but fascinating, offering a glimpse into the diverse geographical tapestry of India. Amara enjoyed the regional food served on the train, starting with spicy Kerala and Konkan cuisine and transitioning to the milder, yet flavorful Gujarati dishes.

Upon reaching Dwarka, Amara took an auto-rickshaw to her hotel, which was conveniently located near the railway station. The hotel, a three-star establishment, stood tall with its modern architecture and welcoming façade. Amara had booked a double occupancy room, which was spacious and well-maintained. The room featured a comfortable queen-sized bed, a small sitting area with plush chairs, and a desk. The decor was simple yet elegant, with warm lighting and soft hues that created a relaxing ambiance. The hotel amenities included a multi-cuisine restaurant where Amara wished to relish both local and continental dishes. She was particularly looking to enjoy the fresh seafood and traditional Gujarati thalis. The staff were courteous and attentive, ensuring her stay was pleasant and hassle-free.

After settling in her room, she called Rakesh and Arvind. Both of them were arriving the next day, while Amara had the whole of the afternoon and evening to herself. She visited the famous Dwarkadhish Temple, explored the local markets, and took a serene walk along the Gomti River. She enjoyed the local street food available in the market. In the evening, Arvind gave a call to check on her.

"Hi Amara, Are you ok?"

"Hi Arvind, Yes I am doing well. Where have you guys reached?" Amara was keen to see both of them.

"We just passed Ahmedabad, we should reach early morning around 5 AM."

"What about others?"

"Raghavan will reach tomorrow. But Gautam is going to be late, either tomorrow night or the day after morning. He had some business deal which he could not skip."

"He hasn't yet trusted his son. Still holding all the reigns." Amara knew about the rift between Gautam and his son.

"Yes, looks like it."

"Anyways, is the item safe?"

"Yes, it is in the safest location."

"Safest location... where?"

"I wore it as a pendant to my necklace, it is sitting on my chest."

"You are crazy. Ok, stay safe, we will meet soon"

"Yes sure, you too."

Amara spent the night in the hotel with eager anticipation to meet her friends Rakesh and Arvind. She had known Rakesh for nearly two decades and Arvind for over a decade. Beyond their shared quest for immortality and uncovering its secrets, she considered both of them to be the closest people she knew in the entire world. As she lay in bed, she cherished her old memories of the first time she met Rakesh and Arvind. As she drifted off to sleep, Amara felt a profound sense of gratitude for the enduring friendships she had with Rakesh and Arvind. These memories and the anticipation of seeing them again filled her heart with warmth and comfort.

The next morning, around 5 AM, Amara's phone rang, waking her from a deep sleep. It was Rakesh. He informed her that they had arrived in Dwarka and had checked into the same hotel. He sounded tired after the early morning hassle. Rakesh mentioned that both he and Arvind needed some rest after the long trip and suggested they meet for breakfast at 10 AM in the hotel lobby. Amara agreed, feeling a rush of excitement. She glanced at the clock and realized she had a few more hours to rest. She lay back down, her mind buzzing with anticipation for the reunion. Memories of their past adventures and discussions about immortality floated through her mind, making it difficult to fall back asleep.

As the morning light began to filter through the curtains, Amara finally drifted off into a light sleep, dreaming of the day ahead. At 9 AM, her alarm went off, and she got up, feeling surprisingly refreshed. She took her time to get ready and wanted to look her best for her friends. By 9:45 AM, she was heading down to the lobby, her heart pounding with excitement. The anticipation of seeing Rakesh and Arvind again filled her with joy, and she couldn't wait to share breakfast and rekindle their deep, cherished friendship.

Amara took both Rakesh and Arvind to a nearby restaurant for a Gujarati breakfast. She had enjoyed the food at the same place the previous evening and wanted her friends to experience it too. They savored the delicious dishes together, relishing the unique flavors and the warm, inviting atmosphere. Amara felt a sense of contentment seeing Rakesh and Arvind enjoy the meal as much as she had.

As they were finishing their delicious Gujarati breakfast, Arvind's phone rang. It was Raghavan, with critical information about his whereabouts. Arvind listened intently, nodding occasionally, while Amara and Rakesh exchanged curious glances. After the call ended, Arvind immediately checked for updates regarding Professor Rao and Gautam's arrivals in Dwarka. He informed Amara and Rakesh that Professor Rao had arrived that same morning and was staying at another hotel property nearby. This news brought a sense of relief to the group, knowing that their esteemed colleague and mentor was already in town. They discussed the possibility of meeting him later in the day to go over their plans.

However, the news about Gautam was less certain. Arvind relayed that Gautam was expected to reach Dwarka either late tonight or early the next morning. This uncertainty left a gap in their immediate plans, but they were hopeful that he would arrive safely and promptly join them. They decided to spend the rest of the morning planning their next steps and coordinating with Professor Rao. Amara felt a mix of excitement and tension, knowing that their quest for immortality was moving forward but also aware of the challenges that lay ahead.

Amara asked Rakesh and Arvind about their families as they met for breakfast. She inquired about their whereabouts and specifically asked about Rakesh's son Ravi's health. Rakesh informed her that Ravi was doing better, and Amara was pleased to hear this. Their conversation included updates on their families, with Amara showing genuine concern and interest.

Arvind's curiosity soared as he gazed upon the gem adorning Amara's neck, dangling delicately from a silver chain. Its intricate design seemed to whisper secrets of ancient mysteries, promising a glimpse into the enigma of immortality. For more than two decades, Arvind had pursued this elusive puzzle, and now, with the gem before him, his excitement bubbled to the surface, mingled with a tinge of emotion. As Amara unveiled the gem to Arvind and Rakesh, the room seemed to hold its breath, caught in the gravity of this momentous revelation. Arvind's heart quickened its pace, his eyes fixed intently on the mystical artifact that could potentially unlock the secrets he had long sought.

With trembling hands, Amara gently handed the gem to Arvind, who accepted it with reverence, as if holding the key to a long-lost kingdom. His fingers traced the intricate patterns etched into its surface, feeling the weight of centuries of history and legend. In that fleeting moment, Arvind felt a surge of emotions overwhelm him – a mixture of joy, anticipation, and perhaps a hint of trepidation. This was it, the culmination of years of tireless pursuit, the turning point in his quest for understanding.

But amidst Arvind's euphoria, Rakesh's voice broke through the reverie, a gentle reminder to maintain composure. Arvind's excitement, while understandable, threatened to overshadow the gravity of the situation. With a nod of understanding, Arvind reluctantly tore his gaze away from the gem, realizing the need to exercise caution and restraint. Reluctantly, he handed the gem back to Amara, though every fiber of his being yearned to continue exploring its secrets. The tantalizing glimpse he had been granted only fuelled his determination to delve deeper into the mystery of immortality.

As Amara secured the gem back around her neck, Arvind's mind buzzed with questions, his curiosity now more fervent than ever. The taste of progress lingered on his tongue, sweet yet tinged with the bitter realization that there was still much ground to cover. With a deep breath, Arvind composed himself, his resolve strengthened by the promise of what lay ahead. The journey towards unraveling the mystery of immortality was far from over, but with the gem as their guide, he knew they were one step closer to uncovering the truth that had eluded them for so long.

"Where do you think we should all meet?" Arvind asked both Rakesh and Amara while sipping a cup of tea in the restaurant and gaining his composure back.

"I think we should meet in a public place which is also secluded. We should avoid places that are monitored by CCTV cameras. Just in case, Raghavan gets into trouble." Rakesh gave his opinion.

"Yes, I also agree with Rakesh. I had visited a few places yesterday, the place near the lighthouse is public yet gives you the privacy you need." Amara recommended.

"Ok, I think we use such a place. Let me inform all about the location. Tomorrow 4 PM sounds ok to you both." Arvind enquiring with both Rakesh and Amara while he started to dial Raghavan.

"Yes, that sounds like a plan." Amara nodded, looking at Rakesh.

Raghavan had received a phone call from Arvind, who urgently requested him to plan a journey from Rameswaram to Dwarka. Arvind had requested Raghavan to bring the conch he had stolen from the temple's secret treasure. Raghavan listened patiently to Arvind and took mental notes about the itinerary. Without wasting time, Raghavan immediately began planning for his trip. He checked the train schedules and booked his tickets for the quickest route available. The next day, he packed his essentials, ensuring he was prepared for the long journey ahead. Raghavan reached the Rameswaram railway station early, with a sense of duty and urgency.

The train ride was long and arduous, but Raghavan remained focused on his mission. He gazed out the window, watching the changing landscapes as the train sped towards its destination. When the train finally pulled into Dwarka, Raghavan took an auto and enquired about a lodge near the seashore to stay. The auto driver took him through the traffic briskly, changing lanes and overtaking fellow auto drivers and cars with ease. Raghavan had never experienced such reckless driving on busy streets where every inch of space was being used by the drivers. He caught on to one of the handles in the auto which helped him maintain balance. After a brisk and eventful ride for a few minutes, the auto stopped in front of a decent two-star hotel which had a busy reception area. The auto driver accompanied Raghavan to the reception to ensure he got the commission for bringing a customer to the hotel. Soon, Raghavan was allotted a single-bed, non-air-conditioned room.

Raghavan checked the room and placed his bag on top of a table, which was placed at one corner of the room. He opened his bag and reached inside, feeling around until his fingers closed around a silk pouch. He opened and checked the Conch was safely placed inside. Satisfied, he set the pouch aside, picked up his phone, and made the call.

"Hello Arvind, I am staying in Sea View Lodge near the beachfront"

"Hello, Raghavan. We have all arrived except Gautam. He will reach out tonight. He has started from Surat and is coming in his vehicle."

"Ok, Arvind. When and where are we going to meet?"

"I am going to discuss with Professor Rao about it and will inform you soon. Have you got the item?"

"Yes, I have got it. It is safe in my bag."

"Wait for my call, I will call you soon."

Raghavan put his phone on charge near his bed and headed to the bathroom to freshen up. It had been a long train journey where he had to change trains a couple of times and had to wait in the railway platforms or waiting rooms for several hours. He changed into a comfortable light blue colored lungi and called the hotel reception for a hot coffee and snacks for room service. He was well obliged by the hotel staff with quick service and tasty food. He was taking a quick nap when his phone buzzed near his bed. He quickly got up and received the call.

"Yes, Arvind."

"We will meet tomorrow near the lighthouse at 4 PM. It is a public place and has some seating area near the shoreline. Bring your item, we will discuss what to do next, and disperse. Have you booked your return ticket?"

"No, I have not. Should I book for the day after?"

"Yes, book it. You can contact your hotel reception, they can help you with some agents who can provide you with confirmed tickets." Arvind provided the guidance which Raghavan was looking for.

"Yes, sure. I will manage it."

"Ok, we will meet tomorrow then."

"Yes."

Professor Rao had meticulously arranged his travel itinerary, booking a flight from Bhubaneswar to Mumbai and scheduling a train ride from Mumbai to Dwarka. Traveling light, he embarked on his journey with a sense of anticipation, eager to meet the group awaiting him in Dwarka. Throughout his travels, he maintained close communication with both Arvind and Gautam, ensuring that they were updated on his progress and any changes in his plans. Their reciprocal communication helped streamline his journey, providing him with reassurance and support along the way.

As the flight soared through the skies, Professor Rao found solace in the breathtaking views outside his window, contemplating the adventure that lay ahead. Upon landing in Mumbai, he seamlessly transitioned to the next leg of his journey, making his way to the train station with practiced efficiency. Despite the hustle and bustle of the crowded terminals, his focus remained unwavering, driven by the prospect of unraveling the secrets of immortality.

The train journey offered a brief respite from the whirlwind of travel, allowing Professor Rao to reflect on the purpose of his trip and the camaraderie he shared with Arvind and Gautam. With each passing mile, anticipation grew, fueling his excitement for the impending reunion. As the train pulled into Dwarka station in the early hours of the morning, Professor Rao felt tired and needed to give his body the much-needed rest.

He had pre-booked a comfortable hotel and took a prepaid taxi to reach his hotel. The hotel staff was swift in the check-in process and in a matter of minutes Professor Rao found himself comfortably relaxing in a double occupancy room where the air conditioning was optimally configured at 21 degrees Celsius. It didn't take much time for Professor Rao to get into a deep sleep. After a few hours of sleep, he found himself fresh and energized as he reached to the side table to check his phone. It was 9 AM, and he ordered himself a hot coffee and a newspaper from the room service. While he engrossed himself in the newspaper, he got a call from Arvind. Their conversation was brief yet meaningful, serving as a reminder of the strong bond they shared and the purpose that brought them together.

Professor Rao had the whole day to himself, so he decided to use it by seeking blessings at the Dwarkadhish Temple. Although he had visited the Dwarka temple around 15 years ago during his completion of the holy pilgrimage of Hinduism, the Chatur Dham, he felt drawn to return.

"*The Dwarkadhish Temple, also known as the Jagat Mandir, holds immense significance in Hinduism, especially concerning the Chatur Dham pilgrimage. Dwarka is believed to be the kingdom of Lord Krishna, a central figure in Hindu mythology and revered as an incarnation of Vishnu. The*

Dwarkadhish Temple itself is dedicated to Krishna, often referred to as Dwarkadhish or the "King of Dwarka". The temple's architecture is a testament to its historical and spiritual importance, with its majestic spires and intricate carvings that date back centuries. For pilgrims, visiting Dwarka is not just about seeing a sacred place; it is about connecting with the divine legacy of Lord Krishna. The temple is said to stand on the very site where Krishna established his kingdom, making it a direct link to his earthly presence. Moreover, the Dwarkadhish Temple is a symbol of devotion and faith, drawing millions of devotees annually. Pilgrims believe that a visit to this temple, along with the other three sites of the Chatur Dham, grants them moksha, or liberation from the cycle of birth and death. "

Professor Rao returned to his hotel after visiting the temple. Settling into the comfortable couch in his room, he decided to call Gautam. When Gautam picked up, he confirmed that he had started from Surat in his car, with his driver. Rao, concerned about his friend's accommodation, asked if Gautam had booked a hotel room for himself. When Gautam admitted that he had not yet done so, Rao offered to help by booking a room in the same hotel where he was staying.

Gautam expressed his gratitude for Rao's assistance. Without wasting time, Rao contacted the hotel reception to inquire about the availability of another room for his friend. The receptionist, recognizing Rao as a current guest, was eager to assist and quickly checked the bookings. After a brief moment, the receptionist confirmed that there was indeed a vacant room available. Rao relayed this information to Gautam, assuring him that a room was secured. Gautam thanked him profusely, relieved that he would have a place to stay upon his arrival. Rao felt a sense of satisfaction knowing that he had helped his friend and ensured his comfort.

At 4 PM, the lighthouse on the shores of Dwarka stood tall against the azure sky, its white structure gleaming in the afternoon sun. The rocky shore below was kissed by gentle waves, creating a soothing, rhythmic sound. Visitors strolled along the elevated pavement that bordered the shore, enjoying the cool sea breeze and the expansive view of the blue ocean. The pavement was dotted with numerous seating areas where people could sit and relax. Families and friends gathered, some chatting animatedly while others sat in quiet contemplation, taking in the serene beauty of the seascape. Children ran along the path, their laughter mingling with the sound of the waves. The scent of saltwater filled the air, adding to the tranquil atmosphere. As the sunlight danced on the water's surface, the scene exuded a peaceful charm, captivating all who were present and offering a perfect moment of relaxation by the sea.

All the members who knew about the secret and formed a small group reached the shore on time. Arvind, Amara, and Rakesh had booked a cab, while Rao and Gautam arrived in Gautam's Audi. Raghavan had taken an auto from his hotel. They all converged at a secluded seating spot near the lighthouse, chosen for its privacy and the scenic view it offered. As they gathered, they greeted each other warmly, their faces lighting up with smiles. It had been a few years since they had last met in person, though they had remained in constant contact over the phone. The joy of reuniting was palpable, and they exchanged hearty handshakes.

Arvind commented on how everyone looked the same, while Amara noted how the sea breeze and the setting sun made the moment even more special. Rakesh brought out a small bag of snacks, and they all settled down, enjoying the food and each other's company. Rao and Gautam shared stories from their journey, and Raghavan updated everyone on his recent adventures. After a few minutes of settling, Arvind started the conversation about the reason they had visited.

"Hello Everyone, thank you for joining us here in a short duration of time. As you all know, we have got a few items which we think might be related to the Secret to Immortality. Raghavan has a Conch, Amara has a gem and Gautam has got a Mace. Can you please show us the pieces?"

On seeing the three ancient relics, the whole group became excited and emotional. Each member felt a surge of awe as they realized they were holding items that might have been touched by Gods. Arvind's hands trembled as he gently picked up one relic, while Amara's eyes filled with tears of reverence. Rakesh, Rao, Gautam, and Raghavan stood in silent admiration, the weight of history and divinity heavy in the air. They exchanged looks of amazement and gratitude, cherishing the profound connection to their heritage and the divine. This moment of shared wonder deepened their bond even further.

"How do we know that these are the ones which hold the secret to immortality? And what else is remaining?" Gautam asked Arvind and Professor Rao, trying to seek the background to these items.

"We had learned in a few of our scriptures and my notebook from forefathers that a few drops of the Amrit had fallen on the earth during the Samudra Manthan. You all know about the story, so I will not go into details. We also understood that Lord Vishnu had cursed these drops, amended them to some items, and took away the power of immortality from individual drops. While he did this, immortality could still be achieved if all the cursed items were put together."

"How can we be sure?"

"We are not sure, Gautam, but there is enough evidence in the research we had done that points to that theory" Professor Rao intervened.

"Yes, let me explain. I inherited a scroll from my grandfather that features a Kalash on the back and several inscriptions accompanied by symbols. The scroll contains eight lines of inscriptions, which we believe might indicate eight locations, eight items, or stories from eight ancestors. At the top of the scroll is a circle, symbolizing either "Shoonya" or "Surya," both of which represent immortality. This also aligns with the story my grandfather told me: the scroll holds the secret to immortality. He had further added that this scroll is one of the cursed items, but we doubt it."

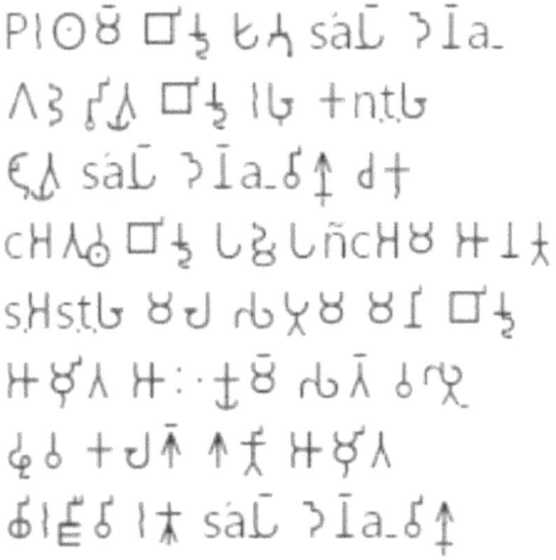

"We have tried to decipher it, based on our knowledge of the ancient scripts and gathering more knowledge from scholars. We understood that the following keywords from the script – curse, Shankha (conch), Gadda (Mace), Mani (Gem), Bindu (drops) and Chiranjeevis."

"Chiranjeevis?" Gautam was perplexed.

"Yes, we were astonished too. We always thought that Chiranjeevis were mythological characters, but we also thought that the Samudra Manthan was also a mythological event. If we are seeking something based on Samudra Manthan, we cannot ignore the presence of Chiranjeevis. So, we started our research about the seven Chiranjeevis."

"Seven Chiranjeevis protecting the seven items!!!" Rakesh correlated the information between the seven drops of Amrit to the seven Chiranjeevis.

"There are millions of Conch, gems, and Mace in our country. How did you know about the location of these items?" Amara has had this question from the beginning of the quest. Arvind had always avoided the question by saying that he would share the answer when the time was right.

"I am also curious about the same, Arvind" Raghavan shared his curiosity.

"Yes, we will reveal everything. Finding the location of these items was the most difficult and time-consuming part of our research." Professor Rao addressed the curiosity around and looked at Arvind.

"After Professor Rao had visited Rameswaram and met with you, I also visited the place a few more times. I went to the temple's library and reached out to multiple people in the admin department along with the main priest."

"You never told me about this Arvind. Professor Rao, did you know about it?" Raghavan was visibly disturbed and looked at the Professor. Professor gestured him to calm down and listen to Arvind.

"My questions always revolved around three items: the conch, the mace, and the gem. During a conversation with the chief priest, I bluffed about a secret treasure hidden within the temple premises. After the vaults of the Padmanabhaswamy temple were opened, all temples grew concerned about their hidden treasures and vaults. The chief priest's reaction revealed to me that there was indeed a hidden treasure in the temple known only to him. I then shared this information with Raghavan, urging him to investigate the chief's secrecy."

"How did you know it was Conch in the temple and not the others?" Amara asked.

"We didn't know. I gave a clue to Raghavan to check the place and find anything on these three items. And by the way, we are not sure if these items are the key to our quest or are just ancient artifacts."

"But it seems too good to be true that your hunch on the Chief's secret resulted in this." Rakesh was not fully convinced about the story.

"You are right. And this was not the only hunch. There have been numerous such hunches. Professor Rao has visited many storerooms, museums, temples, spiritual places, etc. We have extensively traveled. In one of our interactions with a priest in Hampi, he revealed that there were famous craftsmen and stone sculptors who were excellent at creating hidden compartments and vaults that were used by kings to store their secrets. On further investigation, we came to know that there is a family in Kerala who were known for this craft. That is when we came to know about Anandan's family. After gathering this information, we shared it with you, Amara."

"What about Dwarka?"

"I got news from my colleagues in an archaeological department that there is a plan to excavate the ruins of the submerged city of Dwarka. I called Arvind and checked with him if he would be interested. Then we relayed the same information to look for Conch, Mace, or Gem in those excavations" Professor Rao responded.

"It has taken us more than 20 years of persistent effort and research to reach here. We didn't gather the information overnight. We have had hundreds of failures in our journey to date and I am sure we have many in the future. I also asked Rakesh to visit the Ujjain Mahakal temple and gather information about any secrets, Chiranjeevis, and Amrit Kalash. We didn't reach any conclusion, it was a dead end for us."

Everyone had heard the justification around the claims that Arvind had made. He had taken a vital piece of information from his grandfather and had continued to search for pieces to complete the puzzle. On his journey to find these pieces, he met many people and heard hundreds of stories. He never disregarded any of these stories; instead, he kept piling the information and connecting the dots. Through each encounter, Arvind meticulously gathered details, carefully analyzed and cross-referenced them. His determination grew with each revelation, fuelled by the intricate web of knowledge he had amassed. People were intrigued by his dedication and often shared their insights, further enriching his quest. Over time, Arvind's puzzle began to take some shape, with each new piece fitting into his story. Professor Rao's knowledge served as a guiding beacon, illuminating the path forward.

Arvind and Professor went on to share a few of their failed expeditions in the quest to find information about the items that held the secret to immortality. A few years back, their quest took them into the heart of Assam and began with whispers and stories of an ancient manuscript hidden within the depths of the Kaziranga National Park. Local legends shared stories of a scroll that was linked to the elixir of life, safeguarded by nature itself. As they ventured deeper into the park, Arvind and Professor Rao were greeted by a thick, almost impenetrable fog. The dense forest, home to the endangered one-horned rhinoceros, seemed alive with secrets.

After days of navigating treacherous terrain and evading wild animals, they stumbled upon an overgrown temple ruin, partially submerged in a hidden lake. The walls of the temple were adorned with cryptic carvings depicting celestial beings and mystical herbs. Despite their best efforts to decode the inscriptions, they found nothing but fragmented clues suggesting a deeper connection between the forest's flora and the legendary elixir. Exhausted and disheartened, they left Assam, their quest for the scroll thwarted by the enigmatic jungle.

In another such expedition, the snow-clad peaks of the Himalayas were their next destination, driven by tales of a secluded monastery that possessed an ancient alchemical formula. The monastery, perched high on a remote cliff, was said to be guarded by monks who had achieved extraordinary longevity. The journey to the monastery was perilous, with treacherous ice paths and unpredictable weather testing their resolve.

Upon arrival, they were met with an eerie silence. The monks, though welcoming, were reticent about their secrets. Arvind and Professor Rao spent weeks assisting in the monastery's daily rituals, hoping to gain the monks' trust. One night, they were led to a hidden chamber filled with ancient texts. However, the writings were in a script neither of them could decipher. Their hopes were briefly reignited when they discovered a map leading to a hidden valley known as the "Valley of Flowers," reputed to harbor rare medicinal plants.

Their expedition to the valley ended in disappointment. Despite the valley's breathtaking beauty and diverse flora, they found no evidence of the legendary plants. Weighed down by the knowledge that some secrets of the Himalayas might never be uncovered, they returned empty-handed but with a profound respect for the mountain's mysteries.

Their expedition to Odisha focused on the ancient and mysterious temples scattered across the region. The most promising among these was the Konark Sun Temple, a 13th-century marvel known for its intricate carvings and astronomical precision. According to local lore, the temple was originally built by Samba, the son of Lord Krishna, who sought to cure himself of leprosy by worshipping the Sun God. This legend hinted at healing powers—an irresistible draw for anyone seeking immortality. Arvind and Professor Rao pored over ancient texts and consulted with local historians, who spoke of a hidden chamber beneath the temple, said to contain a crystal that could harness the energy of the sun. Descending into the damp, dimly lit passageway, they were met with an array of traps and puzzles, each more perplexing than the last. After hours of navigating through these hazards, they reached a large chamber adorned with frescoes depicting celestial beings and ancient rituals. In the center of the chamber stood a pedestal, upon which rested a rock that had an engraving placeholder that would have once held a gem or crystal. Another episode unveils ancient secrets which resulted in disappointment for both.

Professor Rao recalled another exciting story. Arvind and Professor Rao had embarked on several expeditions to the Ellora Caves, driven by the legend of hidden secrets to immortality. Despite their extensive preparations, each journey ended in enigmatic failure. Their first expedition focused on Cave 16, the magnificent Kailasa temple. Rumors had suggested that beneath the temple's central pillar lay an ancient manuscript detailing the elixir of life. They spent days deciphering the inscriptions and carefully lifting stone slabs, but all they discovered were centuries-old pottery shards and a maze of tunnels leading nowhere. The legend of the manuscript remained just that—a tantalizing myth.

Undeterred, they turned their attention to Cave 10, the Vishvakarma cave, also known as the "Carpenter's Cave." It was said that a secret chamber existed behind the massive Buddha statue. Guided by faint echoes of a hidden door, they meticulously scanned the walls for clues. A hidden lever finally revealed itself, and their hearts raced as the stone door creaked open. Inside, they found a room filled with ancient scrolls. However, the texts were nothing more than astrological charts and herbal remedies—valuable, but not the immortality secret they sought.

Their final and most harrowing adventure took them to the darkest corners of Cave 32, dedicated to the Jain Tirthankaras. Legends whispered of a cursed pool that granted eternal life at a terrible cost. The air grew thick with an unexplainable chill as they navigated through the cave's labyrinthine passages. Deep within, they found the pool, its waters eerily still and dark. Professor Rao dipped a vial into the liquid for analysis. Later, the analysis revealed the water to be toxic and filled with natural poisons from underground seepage.

Despite their failures, each expedition brought them closer to understanding the depths of human history and the lengths to which people would go in their quest for immortality. The Ellora Caves remained an enigma, holding its secrets tightly within its ancient walls.

Throughout their expeditions and research, Arvind and Professor Rao sought help and guidance from a diverse array of experts. Priests shared ancient texts and rituals, while local guides led them through the intricate cave systems. Trekkers provided the physical endurance needed for their journeys, and monks imparted spiritual insights. Archaeologists and geologists offered their knowledge of the caves' history and geological formations. The local tribes shared folklore and legends passed down through generations, enriching their understanding of the caves' mysteries. Each expert contributed a piece to the puzzle, although the ultimate secret of immortality remained elusive.

"What do we do next? How do we know if these items are genuine or not?" Rakesh asked Arvind.

"I have a connection in Varanasi who can do Radiocarbon Dating, Ring analysis, Radiometric Dating, and material analysis of these items, and understand the age of these. It will take a few days to get the data, but that will give us a clear idea of what we are dealing with."

Everyone looked perplexed by the plan and knowledge that Arvind possessed to determine the origin of the items. He could sense that everyone wanted a bit more explanation on these techniques and ideas.

"What are the techniques? How will it solve the mystery?" Gautam asked Arvind.

"Let me explain how we can determine the age of the conch using radiocarbon dating and ring analysis. Firstly, let's delve into radiocarbon dating. Radiocarbon dating relies on the decay of radioactive carbon isotopes in organic materials like shells. As organisms absorb carbon from their environment, including the ocean, they incorporate both stable and radioactive carbon isotopes. When an organism dies, it stops absorbing new carbon, and the radioactive carbon begins to decay at a known rate. By measuring the ratio of radioactive carbon to stable carbon in a sample, we can estimate its age. Now, onto ring analysis. Just like trees have growth rings, conchs also form growth rings as they grow. These rings are visible in cross-sections of the shell. Each ring represents a period of growth, usually corresponding to a year. By combining radiocarbon dating with ring analysis, we can cross-validate our results. Radiocarbon dating gives us an approximate age, while ring analysis provides a more precise estimate by counting the annual growth rings."

Arvind had come prepared.

"Will we follow the same for all the three items?" Amara asked.

"Radiocarbon dating can be done on all the items. In addition to that, we will do Radiometric Dating for the gem that you got, Amara. For the mace, I am not very sure what can give the age, but a thorough material analysis can shed some light on the next steps we can take."

"Sir, can you also shed some light on Radiometric dating?" Rakesh asked with a sarcastic humour.

"Yes students, I will." Arvind replied with a smile. Everyone laughed at this while Arvind continued.

"Radiometric dating is our key to unlocking the age of gems. Here's the drill: we're focusing on isotopes, like carbon-14. When a gem forms, it contains a certain ratio of isotopes. Over time, these isotopes decay at a known rate. By measuring the remaining ratio of isotopes in the gem, we can calculate how long it's been since it formed. This method works for minerals with radioactive isotopes, like uranium-lead dating for zircons."

"Ok, that's enough education for the day. What about the other items which we need to complete the quest?" Gautam was excited with all the progress but was equally anxious about the next steps.

"We have got some more work to do. In a few of the stories, cremation grounds and Kalpavriksha have connections to immortality, we will need to do some research"

"Why cremation grounds?"

"We have heard that the way to gain immortality is by beating death. While logically cremation grounds are not the places where people die, but they are closely associated with Yama. If Yama is pleased, then He might never come for your soul, and hence you may become immortal. These are all stories and folklore that we have gathered so far, but have yet to deep dive on them." Professor Rao explained.

"Interesting concept," Rakesh commented on the Professor's explanation.

Arvind collected the three items with care, delicately placing them inside his bag. He expressed gratitude to each one, acknowledging their significance in the research and quest. Promising to keep them all informed, he assured them of updates from the carbon dating and other techniques. With a sense of responsibility, he embarked on his journey, carrying not just artifacts, but a commitment to uncovering their stories. After bidding farewell, everyone departed from the shores of Dwarka, each heading towards their respective destinations. With memories of the ancient city lingering in their minds, they set off on their journeys, carrying with them the experiences and discoveries from their time by the sea.

Pratham bindu Shankha śāp denā

Gadda Dwitya bindu rahu kaṇṭha

Tritya śāp denā vishnu chakra

Caturtha bindu padma pañcama Ananta

ṣaṣṭha mala saptama mani bindu

Amrita Aikyam sat Vastu

Dhruva Kalash shakti Amrita

Chiranjeevi raksha śāp denā Vishnu

CHAPTER SEVEN

THE TRAP

Vyasa waited for all the Chiranjeevis to convene and discuss the next course of action. He had kept them informed about the events that had unfolded over time. However, the Chiranjeevis were not pleased upon learning that some of the elements had been stolen or gone missing. They expressed their gratitude to Lord Vishnu for cursing each drop of Amrit, ensuring that no single element held the power to grant immortality to humans. Had it been otherwise, it would have caused great distress and unrest among the Devas.

It was time for the next step, to find if the elements were lost or in possession of someone. Either way, the element needed to be brought back. These elements were made out of the drops of Amrit, which had the power of immortality when combined. The elements were cursed but indestructible, that power laid only in the hands of Lord Vishnu.

Vyasa sat at one corner of his humble house in Varanasi and took out his Ghan. He pressed one of the sides of the cube and touched his forehead. Each side of the Ghan represented one of the Chiranjeevis, which, on being pressed, made a telepathy communication. Vyasa had pressed the Ghan to communicate with Hanuman who was in Rameswaram as Amit Vikram.

"Lord Hanuman, as you know we have been bestowed the honor to protect the Secret of Immortality and maintain the balance of this world and the cosmos. We need to find the stolen or lost elements."

Hanuman was walking to the temple to meet the Chief priest when he heard a familiar voice speaking in his mind.

"Sage Vyasa, yes I am searching for leads for my element. I could not reveal more to you but I can promise you that I will be able to find the missing element very soon."

"I have no doubts in you, Lord Hanuman."

"Do you know what will happen if someone has all the three stolen elements in one place? Will it give them any power?"

"I only know that it will not be useful for gaining immortality unless they have all the elements. But I do not know what will happen if three cursed elements from Lord Vishnu are assembled."

"Yes, I think we need to act fast and retrieve them into our possession. If it goes to the wrong hands, it might create chaos"

"I will try to find out what might happen."

Vyasa was filled with curiosity and concern about the possible consequences if the lost elements could somehow grant powers or knowledge that humans were not meant to possess at this time. Before entering a deep meditative Dhyan state to comprehend the repercussions, he wanted to convey this crucial message to King Bali and Ashwatthama.

Vyasa had asked all the remaining Chiranjeevis to keep the elements in their possession and relieve the keepers of their protection duties. He wanted the Chiranjeevis to keep their human identity for a few more days, in case there was a need for help or assistance, the closest Chiranjeevi could reach the location and provide help.

In the celestial realm, Lord Vishnu sat upon his serpent throne, his usually serene visage darkened by a storm of emotions. Upon hearing of the sacrilege, his anger surged like a tempest, shaking the very fabric of the heavens. His eyes, usually filled with compassion, blazed with an otherworldly fury. The cosmic balance had been disrupted, and the theft of sacred secrets was an affront that could not go unpunished.

The earth trembled in response to his wrath. In Rameswaram, the seas rose angrily, waves crashing against the shore with unprecedented ferocity. The once tranquil waters transformed into monstrous waves that swallowed boats and flooded the coastal villages. Fishermen and villagers fled in terror as the ocean, previously a source of sustenance, turned into a churning maw of destruction. Palm trees were uprooted, their long fronds swept away like insignificant twigs. The sound of crashing waves and the terrified cries of people filled the air, a cacophony of nature's fury and human despair.

In Thiruvananthapuram, the skies darkened ominously, as if a shroud of darkness had descended upon the land. The sun was obscured by thick, black clouds that roiled and churned with malevolent intent. Thunder roared like the wrathful voice of the gods, and lightning sliced through the heavens, illuminating the temple spires and city streets in harsh, jagged flashes. Each bolt of lightning struck with deadly precision, setting trees ablaze and causing buildings to smolder. The inhabitants, usually blessed with gentle weather, were struck by an unyielding storm. People huddled in their homes, their prayers to Lord Vishnu filled with desperation and hope for mercy. Rivers overflowed, turning roads into torrents, sweeping away whatever lay in their path.

Dwarka, the ancient city by the sea, faced a sudden and violent storm. The winds howled like banshees, their shrieks mingling with the sounds of crashing waves and the splintering of wood. Trees were uprooted, their mighty trunks thrown aside as if they were mere matchsticks. The sea, usually a placid guardian of the city, became a furious entity, battering the walls of Dwarka with relentless force. Fishing boats were dashed against the rocks, and the docks were obliterated. Markets and homes were torn apart by the gale, their contents scattered to the winds. People clung to each other, seeking refuge in whatever sturdy structure they could find, their hearts heavy with fear.

The catastrophes left the regions reeling, a testament to the severity of the cosmic crime. The world felt the weight of divine displeasure, and the need to restore balance became imperative. The guardians of the secrets, humbled and resolute, vowed to recover the stolen knowledge and appease the mighty Lord Vishnu. Only then could peace be restored to the troubled lands, and the gods' favor regained.

The guardians pressed on with their mission, the storms gradually began to subside, a sign that their efforts were not in vain. The seas in Rameswaram calmed, the skies over Thiruvananthapuram cleared, and the winds in Dwarka gentled. The regions slowly began to recover from the devastation, their people holding onto the hope that peace would be restored to the troubled lands and that the gods' favor would once again shine upon them.

Vyasa was aware of the wrath that the gods could put on mortal beings for trying to imbalance the world. He offered his prayer to Lord Vishnu and asked for his help and trust to get back the possessions. It could have been a trivial deal for Lord Vishnu to get to the elements and pass them onto the Chiranjeevis, but the elements were formed because of his curse. He did not want to be in close quarters to something he had cursed in the past. He blessed Vyasa and asked him to lead the Chiranjeevis in this quest to find the elements.

Vyasa paced the length of his veranda, his mind swirling with concern. The item that Bali had been tasked to retrieve, a sacred relic of immense importance, was missing. Vyasa's heart sank as the weight of the loss settled upon him. This relic was not merely an artifact; it was a key to divine knowledge, a bridge between the mortal realm and the celestial.

Vyasa spoke with a reassuring tone with Bali. "We will find it, Bali. Tell me, how did this happen?"

Bali recounted his investigation. "After discovering the theft, I spoke with Anandan. He mentioned that he had last opened the treasure a few months ago. It was just after the Alpsi festival when he brought Pallavi and her friends to the temple for a visit. He identified them as Amara and Kalpana, friends of his daughter Pallavi. They were the last to be seen near the relic, and Anandan suspects that it might be one of them"

Vyasa frowned, deep in thought. "Amara and Kalpana? What could their motives be?"

Bali shook his head. "I am unsure. They have always been close to Pallavi, and there was never any reason to doubt their loyalty. However, Anandan's words leave little room for doubt."

Determined to uncover the truth, Bali sets out to find Amara and Kalpana. He paid a visit to Kalpana's house, the journey to uncover the truth had begun. Bali found Kalpana's address and discreetly followed her to the nearby temple. He watched as she purchased flowers and incense, her movements graceful and reverent. She seemed completely absorbed in her routine, greeting vendors with a warm smile and a gentle nod. Bali, hiding in the shadows, waited patiently for the right moment. As the crowd began to thin, he saw his chance. With fewer people around, he approached Kalpana, ready to question her without causing a scene, the temple's peaceful ambiance contrasted with the turmoil in Bali's mind as he prepared to uncover the truth.

As Bali observed Kalpana, he noticed her gentle demeanor and unassuming nature. Her simple personality, reflected in her modest clothing and sincere eyes, made him reconsider his suspicions. Bali spun a story about his lost bicycle with a yellow bag from the temple premises when he had come to sell the coconut to the temple administration. Her kind interactions with others and the serene aura she exuded painted a picture of innocence. Bali's doubt grew; could someone so straightforward and sincere be involved in such a grave theft? The more he pondered, the more he felt compelled to look deeper into other possibilities. He didn't want to draw any conclusions without meeting Amara.

Bali next visited Amara's boutique, intent on speaking with her to cross-check the events and uncover the truth. As he entered the boutique, he was greeted by an assistant who informed him that

Amara had traveled out of town for a few days. Disappointed but not deterred, Bali realized he would have to wait for her return to continue his investigation and piece together the missing details.

After a couple of days, when Bali finally met Amara in her boutique, he was struck by an unsettling sensation. As she approached him, a palpable aura of dark energy seemed to radiate from her. The boutique, usually vibrant with colors and fabrics, felt oddly oppressive. Bali maintained his composure, carefully masking his suspicion. The negative energy made him wary; he didn't want to accuse her directly without any evidence. Amara mentioned that Kalpana had contacted her and given her a heads-up about Bali's visit. Bali subtly questioned her about the afternoon the relic went missing, observing her reactions closely and trying to keep the environment as light as possible. Amara answered calmly, but the dark aura around her made Bali more determined to uncover the truth cautiously.

Though Amara maintained her calm, Bali could read the smallest of changes in body language which indicated that Amara was hiding something. Bali wanted to scan her home to check for the lost "Gem", he devised a plan.

The next afternoon when Amara was busy in her boutique, Bali quietly entered Amara's home, determined to uncover the truth about her. He moved silently through the dimly lit rooms until he reached her bedroom. His eyes fell on a wooden almirah, its key conspicuously placed on top. He retrieved the key and unlocked the almirah, where he found a second phone, tucked away. Switching on the phone, Bali quickly scanned its call log. A single number appeared repeatedly, raising his suspicion. He committed the number to memory, knowing it could be a crucial lead. Continuing his search, he opened the drawers beneath the almirah. Among the mundane items, a recent bill from a hotel in Dwarka caught his eye.

The bill, dated just a few days ago, hinted at a connection to her recent travel. Bali carefully noted the hotel's name and date, aware that this discovery could link Amara to the stolen relic and the ensuing chaos, but he was disappointed to not find the "Gem" in her house. With this new information, he left the house as quietly as he had entered, ready to delve deeper into the mystery. His suspicion towards Amara had become deeper.

Bali got in contact with Vyasa to inform him about his suspicion about Amara.

"Sage Vyasa, after meeting Amara, I got a sense of dark and negative energy around her. Although she was very calm and composed while we were having a conversation, I could sense that she was hiding something from me."

"Do you have any leads to find the stolen element?"

"Yes, I scanned her home today. I didn't find the element, but I found a few things which made me suspicious, a mobile phone tucked in an almirah and a hotel bill. The peculiar thing about the phone is that it only had one phone number in all of the call logs."

"That's very unlikely."

"And the hotel bill was for a recent visit to Dwarka."

Hanuman learned about Raghavan's whereabouts from the temple chief after realizing that the element was missing from the temple's secret treasure. Intrigued by Raghavan's mysterious past and recent absence from the temple, Hanuman was curious to know more about Raghavan. The chief shared sadly, how Raghavan was one of the revered priests in the town who was respected and adored by all the people in the town. His knowledge of the ancient scriptures, his storytelling ability and the way he conducted the various religious rituals were second to none. He never had a family but boasted a rich heritage and inheritance from his forefathers, but he never showed any greed for money or wealth. He lived in a humble house and followed a very disciplined lifestyle.

The priest took a deep breath, and with a concerned and sad voice he said, "One night a few years back, I came back to the temple to take my keys which I had kept on a shelf near the main sanctum. I heard some footsteps coming from behind the sanctum. My heart sank when I saw Raghavan coming out of the secret passage that leads to the secret vault. I was shocked seeing his face and could not understand for a moment. The next moment, he started to run outside, which was alarming. I could not run behind him, so I started to scream and shout for the guards and fellow priests who stayed inside the temple premises to get hold of Raghavan. He was caught near the west gate."

"Did he have anything on him?"

"He did hold a shiny silver object, which we later came to know was a Shiv Ling"

"Why would he steal only a silver Shiv ling from a vault? Don't you think it is suspicious?"

"The police and guards searched him thoroughly before taking him to the police station. They only found the Shiv Ling"

"Was he out of your sight when he ran out?"

"Yes, he was out of my sight for a minute."

"Ok, please continue"

He revealed that Raghavan, after being released from jail, decided to leave his life as a priest behind. The burden of his past and the stigma attached to his imprisonment weighed heavily on him, prompting a need for a fresh start. Seeking redemption and a new identity, Raghavan had chosen to open a small store near the shores of Rameswaram. The store, specialized in selling antiques and decor items crafted from seashells. It was Raghavan's way of staying connected to the spiritual and natural beauty of Rameswaram while distancing himself from his troubled past.

With this information, Hanuman felt a mix of relief and resolve. He thanked the chief priest and made his way to the shores, determined to meet Raghavan. Hanuman hoped that this encounter would bring closure to his quest.

Before leaving, Hanuman enquired with the priest.

"I would also like to talk to your son, if you don't mind"

"Yes, of course. I am embarrassed to lose the only sign of your family's history. I am available to help you all the way, Amit"

"Thank you, Guruji." Hanuman realized that he was in his human form and needed to act accordingly.

Hanuman, eager to gather information from Raghavan, immediately headed to the shores of Rameswaram after speaking with the temple chief. He had learned that Raghavan, once a revered priest, had turned his life around by opening a small store selling antiques and decor items made of seashells. Determined to find him, Hanuman introduced himself as Amit and began asking around near the bustling beach market.

Locals, familiar with the area and its inhabitants, directed Hanuman to a corner shop at the end of the market named "Shanti Treasures." Excitement and anticipation built up within him as he navigated through the busy market streets, only to find the shop closed when he arrived. The shutters were down, and there was an air of abandonment surrounding the small, quaint shop. Undeterred, Hanuman began to inquire with the nearby vendors and shopkeepers. They informed him that Raghavan had traveled out of town a few days prior, but no one seemed to know when he would return. Each response Hanuman received chipped away at his hope, replacing it with growing unease.

The uncertainty of Raghavan's return troubled Hanuman deeply. The thought that Raghavan might have left his home, his town, and the temple for good weighed heavily on his mind. If Raghavan had indeed left for an indefinite period, the chances of retrieving the crucial element would be severely hampered.

As he stood in front of the closed shop, Hanuman felt a wave of frustration and anxiety. The journey to Rameswaram had led him to a dead end, and the path forward seemed unclear. Determined not to give up, Hanuman resolved to stay in Rameswaram a bit longer, hoping to find any sign or information about Raghavan's return. This quest had become more complicated than he had anticipated, but Hanuman was not one to abandon a mission easily.

He walked to a secluded part of the beach and tried to make contact with Sage Vyasa using the Ghan, the telepathic mind reading with voice communication system, which was available in the form of a cube with the Chiranjeevis.

"Sage Vyasa, I have got a lead. There was a theft in the temple's secret vault, and the chief priest feels that the thief, Raghavan, might be the one who would have taken it"

"Lord Hanuman, if a human has stolen our element without stealing all the wealth around him, that means he surely knows about the element. He is going to be crucial to solve this whole quest."

"I will find him" Responded with resolve in his voice

"There is a coincidence also here, Lord Hanuman. The suspect after whom King Bali is, was also out of town for a few days, and she returned yesterday. One piece of information that I got from Bali was that she visited Dwarka."

"Ok, Sage Vyasa. This is helpful."

As Hanuman was walking back to the market, he saw a person talking on a mobile phone, a technology that humans used that was far dated for the Chiranjeevis. But this gave him an idea to find the whereabouts of Raghavan. Hanuman asked the neighboring shop to help him contact Raghavan, telling a sympathetic story of how Raghavan had taken money from him and was not picking up his phone. Hearing the sad story, the neighbor rang Raghavan's mobile phone. Hanuman requested him not to reveal anything but rather ask Raghavan about his return and where he was.

"Radhavan Anna, where are you? When are you coming back? Should I sell your shop to someone, Anna?" The neighbour asked in a very jovial manner. He had realized that the humans had pioneered the skill of deceit, something he was ashamed and guilty of doing as well.

"Seri, Anna."

The shopkeeper informed Hanuman that Raghavan was in transit and would reach Rameswaram by tomorrow. He would open his shop the day after. Hanuman was curious to know about the place from where Raghavan was traveling back.

He inquired, "He is going to reach tomorrow, looks like he had gone to a different country!!"

"I don't know, he said someplace in Dwarka. I don't know where it is that?"

"I also don't. But, thank you Anna for the help. Please keep this a secret between us, don't tell him."

"Don't worry, Paa"

Hanuman got some good news, Raghavan was not absconding and secondly, he had gone to visit Dwarka. Now he was concerned that there was a possible link between the theft of two elements. Two suspects visited the same place. He immediately shared this new piece of information with Sage Vyasa and requested him to pass it on to Bali and Ashwatthama.

Bali gave a call to the number. Arvind was startled upon receiving the call. He knew that number was only known to the group, and the sudden call took him by surprise. Despite the initial shock, Arvind decided to ignore it, convincing himself it might just be a coincidence. He shook off the uneasy feeling and tried to focus on his work, but the thought lingered in his mind. Could it be just a coincidence, or was there more to the call than met the eye? Despite his attempts to dismiss the incident, the question gnawed at him throughout the day.

Bali only got the name of Arvind, when he tried to enquire about his location, he sensed that Arvind was not comfortable and got spooked. Arvind picked the phone expecting someone else and was startled by hearing Bali. After the brief interaction, Bali gave the number to Vyasa and asked him to give a call sometime later. Vyasa thought about it and came up with a plan.

"Hello Arvind !!!"

"Yes, who is it?"

"Amara gave me your number, she needs help. Can you please come to her place?" Vyasa throwing the dice.

"What happened to her? Why didn't she call herself?"

"I don't know, I am calling from the hospital. Do you live nearby? Can you come please?"

"No, I don't live near her. I am in Varanasi."

"What happened to her?"

"Don't worry, she is well. I will ask her to call you. Thank you, sir" Vyasa disconnected as soon as he got the required information.

Arvind became anxious and got worried thinking about Amara's health, but he wanted to check by calling Amara's phone personally. He picked up and dialled to her boutique's number.

"Hello Amara"

"Yes, Arvind."

"You are alright? Are you ok?"

"Yes, Arvind. I am ok, what happened to you? Why are you asking me that?"

"I got a call to my other number. A man said that you are in trouble and that you asked me to come to you. He knew my name also. He also knew your name."

"Calm down, Arvind. What happened? Relax and recollect again"

"Yes, ok... now I am getting some clarity, Amara. I got two calls today from two different numbers. The first one was the wrong number, while the second one knew about both of us. He knew we were friends and he knew our names. And now they know that I live in Varanasi too. Something is not right, Amara. Did anyone suspicious meet you yesterday or today?

"A coconut farmer named Ramesh had come to ask about his bicycle theft which happened a few months ago. Now that I recall, he was very specific about his question and it cannot be a coincidence that the day about which he was enquiring was the same day I got the thing."

"Ok, it must be. It is not one person and they are suspicious about it. How did they come to know my other number? Someone knows something about our plan. Let me alert others about this, they might reach others too to get more information"

"Yes, you must."

"Ok, we will talk later."

Arvind saved both the numbers on his mobile to investigate in the future. The important thing at hand was to ensure that the items were safe and everyone held their secret. He spoke to Professor Rao, Rakesh, and Raghavan. They all confirmed that they didn't get any calls or had any suspicious interactions with anyone recently. Arvind assured them that he would take care of the situation and keep them posted on any new findings. He gazed at the two numbers he had saved in his phone for some time to gauge the situation on hand.

Professor Rao immediately dialed Gautam to pass on the message that Arvind had just dropped to the group. After a couple of rings, Gautam picked up.

"Hello, Professor Sir. How are you?"

"Gautam, Arvind had just called me. He wanted to alert us that some people might know about our plans and might come to us with stories and deceit to get some information from us. Have you had any suspicion recently?"

"Oh No, Professor!!!" Gautam was stunned and could not fathom how to react to Professor Rao. He had committed something regrettable.

Ashwatthama's journey to uncover the stolen artifact from the submerged city of Dwarka had taken him through a labyrinth of intrigue and deception. His investigation led him to discover that a recent excavation by the marine department had unearthed numerous relics from the ancient city. Determined to retrieve the missing artifact, Ashwatthama delved deeper into the details of the excavation, seeking out those who had been directly involved.

After a couple of days of meticulous inquiry, Ashwatthama identified several officials who had been responsible for cataloging and storing the relics in various store rooms and museums. Among these officials was a particularly suspicious character, a corrupt assistant named Rajesh. Rajesh had a reputation for being easily swayed by bribes and was known to have a lifestyle that far exceeded his modest official salary. Sensing an opportunity, Ashwatthama decided to focus his efforts on Rajesh, believing that he might hold the key to uncovering the truth.

Under the guise of a wealthy collector interested in acquiring ancient artifacts, Ashwatthama approached Rajesh. He engaged him in conversation, subtly probing for information. It didn't take long for Rajesh's greed to surface. Ashwatthama could see the glint of avarice in his eyes, and he knew he was on the right track. Plying him with promises of riches, Ashwatthama gradually gained Rajesh's confidence. For a few meetings, Rajesh began to let slip bits and pieces of information about the excavation and the subsequent handling of the relics.

Rajesh showed a counterfeit mace artefact to Ashwatthama, trying to sell it as the genuine relic. He boasted about its supposed authenticity, emphasizing its historical significance and rarity. However, Ashwatthama, with his deep knowledge of ancient artifacts, quickly realized that it was not the real piece. The craftsmanship was too crude, the engravings lacked the intricate details of the original, and the weight was off.

Ashwatthama pretended to be interested, asking questions and feigning admiration for the counterfeit mace. He wanted to see how far Rajesh would go to deceive him. Rajesh continued his charade, unaware that his ruse had been detected. Ashwatthama decided to confront Rajesh later, but for now, he played along to gather more information. Inside, he felt a mix of anger and determination, knowing he was closer to uncovering the truth behind the stolen artifact.

The next evening, over dinner, Rajesh finally broke. The alcohol had loosened his tongue, and he revealed a crucial piece of information. "You know, there was this one guy, Gautam," Rajesh slurred, his eyes unfocused. "He's the one who paid me off. Wanted something specific. A mace, I think it was."

Ashwatthama's heart quickened at the mention of Gautam and the mace. He pressed Rajesh for more details, trying to extract every bit of information. Rajesh, now completely drunk, continued to babble. "Yeah, Gautam... He was willing to pay a lot. Didn't ask questions, just handed over the money and took the mace. Said it was important to him, something about family heritage or some other nonsense."

With Rajesh's confession, Ashwatthama had a name and a motive. He left Rajesh in his stupor and set about finding Gautam. It wasn't long before he tracked Gautam down to a lavish mansion in the heart of Surat city. He shared this news with Vyasa.

"Sage Vyasa, I have got a good lead to the stolen element." Ashwatthama shared all the events and people involved in the act of stealing the ancient element.

"Ashwatthama, did these all take place in Dwarka?"

"Yes, why do you ask Sage Vyasa?"

"Lord Hanuman and King Bali are also investigating their lost elements. In their investigation, they found that both their leads had traveled to the city of Dwarka in the last few days. It cannot be a coincidence that all the events are in some way connected to the city of Dwarka. It is of major concern; two suspects visit the same place where the third element was lost."

"Yes, I agree. This means all the elements that are stolen are a planned event, and they might be doing it for immortality. So, it is no more a secret that a few drops of Amrit had fallen to earth, they were cursed by Lord Vishnu to some symbolic objects, and if they collect all that they will have access to immortality."

"I don't think they know everything but they have got their hands on some important information."

"Ok, Sage Vyasa. I think it is time we all work together to find the elements and bring them to safety."

"Yes, Ashwatthama. Let's device a plan and we will be in contact soon. You please carry on with your investigation to procure your element."

Ashwatthama traveled to Surat with a cunning plan in mind. Ashwatthama's approach was subtle yet deceptive, designed to unravel Gautam's secrets while posing as an ally. Posing as an artifact and gems collector, Ashwatthama managed to secure a meeting with Gautam.

Upon meeting Gautam, Ashwatthama feigned a friendly demeanor. He mentioned Rajesh, a mutual acquaintance, who he claimed had sold Gautam a counterfeit mace. This immediately put Gautam on edge. Sensing Gautam's discomfort, Ashwatthama delved deeper into his fabricated story, describing how he had been deceived by Rajesh. He portrayed Rajesh as a dishonest dealer who kept the original artifacts for himself, selling fakes to unsuspecting clients.

Gautam, wary and defensive, initially denied any involvement with ancient artifacts, especially anything resembling a mace. His denial was firm, and his demeanor suggested that he was hiding something. Ashwatthama, undeterred, continued to weave his tale, strategically presenting Gautam as a victim seeking justice rather than confrontation. He expressed a deep frustration with Rajesh's alleged deceit, which resonated with Gautam's fears of being exposed.

To further gain Gautam's trust, Ashwatthama produced a mace from his bag, claiming it to be an original artifact of great value. He had obtained the mace through a legitimate source, ensuring its authenticity. The sight of the mace visibly intrigued Gautam, who couldn't hide his interest despite his earlier denials. Ashwatthama emphasized the rarity and historical significance of the mace, painting a vivid picture of its esteemed origins.

Gautam, lured by the allure of possessing an original artifact, began to soften. His curiosity got the better of him, and he examined the mace with a keen eye. Ashwatthama's meticulous descriptions and apparent knowledge of ancient artifacts further convinced Gautam of the mace's authenticity. Slowly, Gautam's defenses crumbled, and he admitted a grudging admiration for the artifact before him.

Realizing he had Gautam hooked, Ashwatthama skilfully shifted the conversation. He implied that Gautam, like many others, might have been a victim of Rajesh's fraudulent dealings. Ashwatthama's insinuations were subtle, yet they planted seeds of doubt in

Gautam's mind. Gautam, desperate to believe he wasn't alone in his predicament, began to open up. He confessed his frustration with Rajesh, hinting at his encounters with potentially counterfeit artifacts.

Capitalizing on this newfound trust, Ashwatthama proposed a deal. He offered to sell Gautam the original mace at a reasonable price, as a gesture of goodwill and solidarity against Rajesh's deceitful practices. Gautam, eager to own an authentic piece and perhaps redeem himself from any prior missteps, agreed to the purchase. Ashwatthama's strategic manipulation had worked; Gautam's involvement was now confirmed.

With the transaction complete, Ashwatthama pressed further, asking about the counterfeit mace that Rajesh had supposedly sold Gautam. He revealed that he indeed possessed a mace he had suspected to be fake. He described how he had acquired it from Rajesh under the pretense of it being an original, and how he had harbored doubts about its authenticity ever since.

Ashwatthama, concealing his satisfaction, offered to inspect the counterfeit mace. He assured Gautam that his expertise could definitively determine its authenticity. Gautam, eager for validation, agreed but he no longer possessed the artifact. He confessed that he had given it to one of his friends and would soon gain possession of it. Ashwatthama tried to find the person and place where Gautam had kept the element. He kept asking subtle questions, "Can you order it from your factory?", "Will it be here in a couple of hours?", "Does your son have it?". The barrage of such questions gave tiny bits of information about the location of the element, it was Varanasi.

By the end of their encounter, Ashwatthama had successfully exposed Gautam's involvement in dealing with the element. Gautam, now convinced of Rajesh's deceit and feeling vindicated by Ashwatthama's support, believed he had found an ally. Little did he know, he had played right into Ashwatthama's hands, revealing the very secrets Ashwatthama had come to uncover.

Ashwatthama came out of Gautam's house after spending a good part of the day with him and wanted to inform Vyasa that the element might be in possession of someone in Varanasi.

"Sage Vyasa, I have got some important information. The suspect, Gautam, had the element till a few days back, but he gave it to someone recently to hold its possession for some reason. I don't have a name for that person, but that person is in Varanasi"

Sage Vyasa could connect the dots now.

"His name is Arvind"

CHAPTER EIGHT

Swap and Secure

Vyasa knew that the epicentre of the quest, which was planned by the mortals, was in Varanasi, and he had concluded that someone named Arvind was leading the adventure for the group. Determined to learn more, Vyasa began his investigation in the ancient city, asking around discreetly to avoid drawing unnecessary attention. He started his inquiry at the local libraries and bookstores, where scholars and enthusiasts of ancient scriptures often gathered. Vyasa spoke to the owners and patrons, subtly mentioning Arvind's name. The responses he received confirmed Arvind's reputation. Many people recognized the name immediately, speaking highly of Arvind's extensive knowledge and passion for ancient texts.

Vyasa then visited a renowned antique shop known for its rare collections. The shopkeeper, an elderly man with a keen interest in historical artifacts, nodded knowingly when Vyasa mentioned Arvind. "Ah, Arvind," he said, his eyes lighting up. "He is a famous collector. His knowledge of ancient scriptures is unparalleled. I knew his father and grandfather also, their family is known to collect and sell antique items, books, and scriptures. Mishra family's warehouse is just two blocks from here."

Vyasa decided to call in the Chiranjeevis, the immortal beings, to meet in Varanasi. Each of these legendary figures held unique wisdom and strength, essential for the success of the quest to get back the stolen elements. With a sense of urgency, Vyasa sat in a secluded place near the banks of the Ganga and used his Ghan to send the message to each Chiranjeevi by telepathy. Everyone got the message and acknowledged back to Vyasa.

As each Chiranjeevi converged towards Varanasi, Vyasa awaited their arrival with a mix of anticipation and relief. He knew that with these immortal beings by his side, the quest stood a greater chance of success. The sacred city of Varanasi, steeped in history and spirituality, would once again witness the gathering of legendary figures, ready to undertake a mission of profound significance.

Upon arriving in Varanasi, each Chiranjeevi made their way to a predetermined meeting point. They reunited with Vyasa, their identities kept secret from those around them. The ancient city of Varanasi, with its labyrinthine streets and timeless aura, provided the perfect backdrop for their clandestine gathering. United once more, they prepared to delve into the mystery that had drawn them together, their resolve steeled by the journey and the purpose that lay ahead.

Vikas Khanna, a brilliant scientist at the IUAC in Delhi, had been a close friend of Arvind since their college days. Their friendship had grown over the years, rooted in their shared passion for ancient history and scientific exploration. Arvind needed carbon dating for the artifacts. Remembering his old friend Vikas, he decided to reach out to him for help.

After arriving in Varanasi, Arvind immediately called Vikas. The phone rang for a few moments before Vikas answered with his familiar, enthusiastic tone. Arvind quickly explained his situation, detailing the significance of the artifact and his urgent need for precise carbon dating. Arvind ensured he kept the secret quest to immortality hidden from him, he emphasized that these artifacts would become of high value if he could prove their age through carbon dating. Vikas listened attentively, recognizing the excitement and urgency in Arvind's voice. He knew how important this project was to Arvind.

Without hesitation, Vikas agreed to help. He owed Arvind a significant favor; years ago, when Vikas had been in a tough spot, Arvind had extended a helping hand without a second thought. It was a difficult period in Vikas's life, both professionally and personally. Arvind's support had been a beacon of hope, and Vikas had never forgotten it.

Arvind felt a wave of relief wash over him. He had been anxious about the possibility of securing the carbon dating analysis, knowing how crucial it was for his research. Vikas assured him that he would handle everything. He instructed Arvind to send the artifact samples to the IUAC in Delhi as soon as possible. He promised to do the carbon dating, but could not promise on the urgency. He wanted a few weeks from Arvind to analyze and provide the report.

The Chiranjeevis goal was to manipulate Arvind's priorities subtly, steering him away from his original plan without arousing suspicion. To achieve this, they devised an elaborate ruse that involved an archaeological and symbol expert from the United Kingdom, whose sudden presence in Kolkata became the centerpiece of their scheme.

The Chiranjeevis began by planting a story about Dr. Alistair Whitaker, a renowned archaeological expert specializing in ancient Indian civilizations and cryptic symbolism. Dr. Whitaker was portrayed as a man of extraordinary skill, with a niche expertise in decoding ancient scripts and artifacts that had baffled historians for decades. His recent discovery of a rare artifact in the ruins of Bengal had brought him to Kolkata, and he was scheduled to leave the country in just two days. The Chiranjeevis ensured that this information reached Arvind through a trusted yet seemingly neutral source—a colleague who casually mentioned Dr. Whitaker's visit during a conversation.

Arvind, who was deeply invested in the quest to uncover the secrets, found the news electrifying. Dr. Whitaker's expertise aligned perfectly with Arvind's needs. The expert was said to possess an unparalleled ability to interpret obscure symbols and connect them to historical events, a skill that could provide Arvind with the missing pieces of his puzzle. The urgency of the situation—Dr. Whitaker's imminent departure—added a layer of pressure, making it seem imperative for Arvind to meet him immediately.

The Chiranjeevis carefully orchestrated the details of the story to make it believable. They fabricated a credible online presence for Dr. Whitaker, complete with academic papers, interviews, and a recent news article about his visit to Kolkata. They even arranged for a fake meeting invitation to be sent to Arvind, ostensibly from Dr. Whitaker's assistant, suggesting a brief window of availability the next day. The invitation emphasized the exclusivity of the meeting, noting that Dr. Whitaker was only meeting a select few individuals due to his tight schedule.

To further sell the ruse, the Chiranjeevis planted subtle clues in Arvind's environment. A local newspaper left on a café table featured a small article about Dr. Whitaker's lecture at a prestigious Kolkata institution. A passerby mentioned the expert's name in a conversation overheard by Arvind. These carefully placed breadcrumbs created an illusion of serendipity, making Arvind feel as though encountering Dr. Whitaker was fate.

As Arvind became increasingly convinced of the importance of meeting Dr. Whitaker, there was the final element: the logistical challenge. Arvind, torn between his desire to meet Dr. Whitaker and his commitment to take the elements to Vikas, decided to compromise. The Chiranjeevis' plan was a masterclass in manipulation, blending psychological insight with meticulous planning.

Arvind was deeply contemplating whether to send the artifacts by courier or to personally take them to Vikas, given their immense significance. He weighed the pros and cons of each option. Sending them by courier would be quick and convenient, allowing him to visit Kolkatta and meet Dr. Whitaker. However, the thought of entrusting such precious items to a third party made him uneasy. He feared potential mishandling or loss during transit, which could jeopardize his entire quest. On the other hand, taking the artifacts to Vikas himself would ensure their safety and allow him to personally oversee their transfer. He could also discuss the project in detail with Vikas and gain immediate insights. However, this option required time and effort, and he would lose the opportunity to meet the expert.

While contemplating this decision, Arvind heard a buzz from his bag. His secret second mobile phone was ringing, displaying an unrecognized number. Despite the unfamiliarity, he decided to pick up the call. It turned out to be the wrong number; the caller was looking for someone else. Although this piqued his curiosity, he thought it might be an honest mistake and decided to ignore it.

Arvind wanted to consult with Professor Rao about whether he should courier the items or take them to Delhi himself. He called Professor Rao, who listened carefully to his concerns. Rao consoled him, understanding the weight of the decision. He advised Arvind to courier the package, reasoning that the artifacts would be in an unknown place with unknown people for a few weeks regardless. Rao emphasized the importance of taking a leap of faith in such situations. After their discussion, Arvind felt reassured. Trusting Rao's judgment, he decided to proceed with sending the package by courier, confident that it was the best course of action given the circumstances. He decided that he would courier the package tomorrow to Vikas's house.

After a brief call from Professor Rao, Gautam felt an overwhelming sense of helplessness after he fell into the trap of a cunning stranger. This person had tricked him into divulging far more information than he should have. The ordeal left Gautam anxious and regretful, plagued by thoughts of what could happen next. He couldn't shake off the feeling that his quest might be irreversibly altered because of his carelessness.

Feeling the need to confide in someone he trusted, Gautam decided to share everything with Professor Rao. The professor had always been a mentor to him, offering guidance and wisdom whenever Gautam faced challenges. As soon as Professor Rao answered the call, Gautam poured out his heart, his voice trembling with remorse. He narrated the entire incident, from the initial friendly conversation with the stranger to the moment he realized he had been duped.

Gautam recounted how the stranger had seemed so genuine and persuasive, coaxing him into revealing information bit by bit. He explained how the stranger's manipulative tactics had preyed on his inherent trust and a momentary lapse in judgment. Gautam admitted that part of his downfall had been fuelled by greed, as the stranger had dangled promises of lucrative opportunities and easy gains. This allure had clouded his better judgment, leading him to ignore the red flags that, in hindsight, seemed so obvious.

"I should have known better, Professor," Gautam said, his voice heavy with regret. "I let my greed get the better of me, and now I might have to pay a heavy price for my foolishness. I'm so sorry for my carelessness."

Professor Rao listened patiently, his silence punctuated by the occasional empathetic murmur. When Gautam finished, there was a pause before the professor spoke. His voice was calm and reassuring, a stark contrast to Gautam's turmoil.

"Gautam, we all make mistakes," Professor Rao began. "What's important is that you recognize where you went wrong and learn from this experience. Greed and carelessness are human traits, but acknowledging them is the first step toward overcoming them. We will figure out what steps we need to take next to mitigate any potential damage. Remember, this is not the end. It's a lesson."

The professor's words provided a sliver of comfort to Gautam. Though he still felt the weight of his actions, knowing that Professor Rao didn't judge him harshly and was willing to help him navigate the aftermath brought a sense of relief. Gautam knew he had a long road ahead to rectify his mistake, but with Professor Rao's guidance, he felt a renewed determination to move forward and act more wisely in the future.

Professor Rao conveyed the whole episode about Gautam falling prey to a scam to Arvind. As he narrated the details of the incident, Arvind listened intently, his brow furrowing deeper with each passing moment. Gautam's unfortunate experience confirmed what Arvind had suspected for some time. After hearing about how the stranger had tricked Gautam into revealing sensitive information, Arvind felt a jolt of realization. This incident wasn't just a random act of deceit; it was part of a larger scheme. Arvind had a hunch that someone was attempting to hijack their quest, and this new development only solidified his suspicions.

Determined yet wary, Arvind decided to personally take the parcel to the courier service. He carefully packaged the samples, ensuring they were secure for the journey. He contacted a reliable courier service and arranged for a swift delivery to Delhi. As he approached the counter, a nagging sense of unease gripped him. He couldn't shake the feeling that something was amiss, that perhaps the parcel might be intercepted or tampered with.

After a moment of hesitation, Arvind decided against sending it. He quietly left the courier service, parcel in hand, and returned home. His instincts told him to wait, to reconsider his strategy. The stakes were too high, and Arvind knew he had to be meticulous and patient to protect the precious contents and their significance.

The Chiranjeevis had started to keenly follow every move of Arvind. They observed his hesitation at the courier service and his cautious return home with the parcel. Every action he took was scrutinized, as they understood the importance of his decisions in their quest. Their vigilance was unwavering, ensuring they were always one step ahead, ready to intervene if necessary.

Arvind stood in his dimly lit study, the parcel resting on his desk. His thoughts were a whirlwind of anxiety, doubt, and determination. He had delayed sending the items once already, and the weight of that decision hung heavily on him. The recent unsettling events had made him acutely aware of the stakes involved. Arvind knew that each step he took could have profound implications for their quest. He paced the room, the parcel constantly drawing his gaze. It was as if the items within held a magnetic pull, reminding him of their significance. The contents were not just relics; they were pieces of a larger puzzle, a puzzle that his grandfather had dedicated his life to. The responsibility of protecting and passing on this legacy now rested squarely on Arvind's shoulders.

As he contemplated his next move, a surge of courage welled up within him. He knew he couldn't afford to let fear dictate his actions. Summoning his resolve, he decided it was time to send the parcel to Vikas, trusting that the items would be handled with the care they deserved. With renewed determination, Arvind wrapped the parcel securely and headed to the courier service once more. As he approached the counter, his mind raced with thoughts of potential risks and the importance of ensuring the package's safe delivery. He paid the courier service, watching intently as the clerk processed the parcel. He marked it as "Delicate," ensuring that it would be handled carefully throughout its journey.

Taking the receipt and the slip, Arvind left the courier office, a mix of relief and apprehension coursing through him. He made his way to one of the ghats in Varanasi, seeking solace and peace of mind. The ghats, with their ancient steps descending into the sacred waters of the Ganges, had always been a place of reflection and tranquillity for him.

As he sat by the river, the gentle sound of the flowing water began to soothe his troubled mind. The city's timeless aura and the serene ambiance of the ghat provided a much-needed respite from the turmoil that had plagued him. He watched as pilgrims and locals performed their rituals, finding comfort in the continuity of life and tradition that Varanasi embodied.

Despite the lingering worries, Arvind felt a sense of clarity slowly emerging. He knew he had done what was necessary, placing his trust in Vikas and the importance of their quest. The journey ahead was uncertain, but he took solace in the fact that he was not alone. As the sun began to set, casting a golden hue over the sacred river, Arvind closed his eyes and took a deep breath. He knew the road ahead would be challenging, but in that moment of tranquility, he found the courage to face whatever lay ahead. Vyasa plotted a plan to swap the package in the courier facility.

Arvind informed Professor Rao about the dispatch of the parcel, explaining that he had finally sent the crucial items to Vikas. Afterward, Arvind contacted Vikas, providing him with the tracking details of the parcel. He explained the significance of the items and the need for their careful handling.

"Please acknowledge receipt of the parcel immediately," Arvind requested, his voice reflecting both urgency and trust. "Also, send me pictures of the items as soon as you receive them. We must ensure everything is intact."

Vikas, recognizing the seriousness in Arvind's tone, promised to keep a close watch on the parcel's progress. He assured Arvind that he would confirm its arrival and share the requested images without delay. This communication provided Arvind with some relief, knowing that Vikas was as dedicated to the mission as he was. Having taken these steps, Arvind felt a bit more at ease. He knew that the parcel was now out of his hands.

Bali, Vyasa, and Parshuram meticulously planned their visit to the courier service shop where Arvind had deposited his parcel. Disguised to blend seamlessly into the bustling streets of Varanasi, each of them took on a role that would allow them to execute their mission without drawing undue attention.

Bali, dressed as a coconut seller, positioned himself just outside the shop, his cart laden with fresh coconuts. He called out to passersby, attracting a small crowd and creating a subtle distraction. His friendly demeanor and persuasive sales pitch drew several customers, keeping the entrance to the shop lively and busy.

Vyasa, disguised as a wandering sage, entered the shop with an air of serene authority. He engaged the clerk in a deep conversation about ancient scriptures and the significance of certain rituals. The clerk, intrigued by the sage's knowledge and presence, became engrossed in the discussion, temporarily forgetting about his other duties.

Parshuram, posing as a potential client, entered the shop shortly after Vyasa. He inquired about the various services offered by the courier company, asking detailed questions about packaging, delivery times, and insurance options. His relentless questioning required the clerk's full attention, further ensuring that the clerk remained occupied.

Meanwhile, Hanuman, disguised as a young man, slipped into the shop unnoticed. His eyes scanned the room, quickly locating the door to the storeroom where all the parcels were kept. Moving with the grace and agility that only he possessed, Hanuman entered the storeroom, careful to avoid making any noise that might alert the clerk.

Once inside, Hanuman unleashed his superpowers, scanning the room with incredible speed and precision. His eyes glowed faintly as he meticulously examined each parcel, his superhuman abilities allowing him to sort through the packages at an astonishing rate. Within moments, he found the parcel that Arvind had sent. He made a clean cut on the parcel and extracted the three items which were carefully wrapped in a plastic bag. Vyasa had requested Hanuman, Bali, and Aswatthama to bring fake replicas of their stolen elements so that they could swap with the originals.

Hanuman quickly exited the storeroom, closing the door behind him as silently as he had entered. He re-joined the bustling street outside, his mission accomplished without a hitch. Bali, still selling coconuts, caught his eye and gave a subtle nod, acknowledging that the task had been completed. Vyasa and Parshuram, sensing that it was time to wrap up their distractions, concluded their conversations with the clerk. The sage imparted a final blessing, and the potential client expressed his gratitude for the clerk's assistance, promising to return soon.

The team regrouped a short distance from the shop near the banks of the Ganga, exchanging brief, triumphant glances. Hanuman reported that he had located the parcel and completed the swap successfully. Each member felt a surge of relief and accomplishment. Vyasa nodded approvingly, Bali grinned, and Parshuram patted Hanuman on the back. Their coordinated effort had paid off, and they were now one step closer to ensuring the safety of the critical items. With their mission for the day accomplished, they silently acknowledged their success and prepared to move forward.

CHAPTER NINE

SECRET UNFOLDS

Vikas received the parcel sent by Arvind. Upon opening the parcel, Vikas discovered three items inside. He promptly called Arvind to confirm that the parcel had arrived safely and to acknowledge the receipt of the three items. Eager to ensure everything was in order, Arvind requested Vikas to send him a picture of the contents.

Vikas complied with the request and took a clear picture of the items. He then sent the image to Arvind. After receiving the picture, Arvind examined it carefully. Seeing the contents of the parcel exactly as he had sent them, he felt a wave of relief wash over him. The anxiety he had been feeling about the parcel's safe arrival and the integrity of its contents dissipated instantly.

Vikas, determined to conduct a carbon dating test on the three artifacts he had received, knew the importance of handling these items with the utmost care. His primary concern was to ensure that he did not damage the artifacts during the testing process. Recognizing the delicate nature of these historical items, Vikas meticulously prepared for the test, gathering all necessary precautions and ensuring he had the right tools and conditions in the lab to conduct the procedure safely.

Despite the urgency he felt, Vikas did not want to make the testing official. The artifacts were of significant importance, and he preferred to keep the test under wraps until he was sure of the results. To create the opportunity to use the lab without raising suspicions, Vikas devised a plan. He decided to make an excuse to re-run a few tests for some official items he was already working on. This strategy allowed him to secure the needed lab time without drawing attention to his true purpose.

In the days that followed, Vikas found pockets of free time in the lab schedule. During these periods, he carefully set up his equipment and prepared the artifacts for testing. Each step was executed with precision, ensuring that the artifacts remained undamaged. Vikas handled the items with gloves and used non-invasive techniques to collect samples for carbon dating. He made sure that his colleagues believed he was merely refining his data on the official projects.

The covert nature of his work added an extra layer of complexity, but Vikas managed to navigate these challenges skillfully. His dedication to both his scientific integrity and the preservation of the artifacts drove him to ensure that his methods were sound and his results accurate. Throughout the process, Vikas maintained his usual professional demeanor, ensuring that his unofficial project did not interfere with his official responsibilities. By the end of the testing phase, Vikas felt confident that he had conducted the carbon dating tests effectively and without compromising the integrity of the precious artifacts.

Vikas had conducted the carbon dating process with a clear plan to handle each of the three distinct artifacts: a conch, a gem, and a metal mace. Each item required a unique approach due to their different compositions and histories.

Firstly, Vikas focused on the conch, which was an organic material and most suitable for carbon dating. He carefully cleaned the conch to remove any surface contaminants that might skew the results. Using a fine scalpel, he scraped off a tiny amount of the conch's material, ensuring that the sample was representative of the original artifact and not affected by any recent contamination. The sample was then treated with an acid wash to eliminate any secondary carbonates that might have formed over time. After this purification process, Vikas combusted the sample in a vacuum-sealed chamber to convert it into carbon dioxide. This carbon dioxide was then analyzed using an accelerator mass spectrometer (AMS), which allowed him to measure the ratios of carbon isotopes and determine the age of the conch.

Next, Vikas turned his attention to the gem. Gems, being inorganic, do not contain carbon and thus cannot be dated directly using carbon dating. However, Vikas knew he could analyze any organic material trapped within the gem or on its surface. He inspected the gem under a microscope and found tiny inclusions of organic matter. Carefully extracting these inclusions using micro-drilling techniques, he treated the organic material similarly to the conch sample. This organic material was combusted and the resultant carbon dioxide was analyzed using AMS. The data provided an approximate age of the organic inclusions, offering insights into the period during which the gem might have been utilized or modified.

Finally, Vikas addressed the metal mace. Metals themselves cannot be dated using carbon dating; however, he could examine any organic residues or corrosion products that had formed on its surface. Vikas meticulously cleaned the mace, searching for organic materials such as wooden handles, leather wrappings, or plant fibers that might have been part of the mace's construction. He found remnants of what appeared to be leather, possibly from a grip or strap. Using the same careful sampling and preparation techniques, he isolated the organic material and prepared it for AMS analysis. This provided an approximate age for the organic components associated with the mace.

Throughout the process, Vikas took meticulous notes and documented each step with photographs and detailed records. He ensured that all samples were handled with the utmost care to prevent contamination. By maintaining strict adherence to protocol and employing advanced techniques, He was able to gather reliable data on the age of each artifact. His careful and methodical approach ensured that the carbon dating results would be both accurate and informative, contributing valuable information to the understanding of these historical objects.

After performing the carbon dating on the three artifacts – the conch, the gem, and the metal mace – Vikas analyzed the reports with a mix of anticipation and trepidation. As he scrutinized the data, a stark and disheartening conclusion emerged: all three items were fake. The conch, which should have shown an age of several centuries, appeared to be only a few decades old. The organic inclusions within the gem and the leather remnants from the mace were similarly recent, far younger than their supposed historical origins.

Vikas immediately picked up his phone and called Arvind to share the bad news. As soon as Arvind answered, Vikas could hear the hopeful curiosity in his voice. "Arvind, I have the results," Vikas began, his tone serious. "I'm afraid the news isn't good. The tests indicate that all three items are modern replicas."

There was a moment of stunned silence on the other end of the line before Arvind responded, his voice filled with disbelief and frustration. "That can't be right, Vikas. These artifacts are supposed to be centuries old. There must be some mistake in your analysis."

Vikas, expecting this reaction, remained calm and understanding. "I understand how you feel, Arvind. I double-checked everything. The conch, the gem, and the mace – all the results point to the same conclusion. They are much younger than we believed."

Arvind, not ready to accept this, argued vehemently. "Are you sure you didn't miss something? Maybe there's been a contamination or an error in the procedure. These items have been authenticated before!"

Vikas took a deep breath, recognizing Arvind's frustration and disappointment. "I assure you, Arvind, I took every possible precaution to avoid contamination. I used the most advanced techniques and followed strict protocols. Let me explain the process and the findings in detail."

He explained Arvind through each step of the carbon dating process. He described how he had meticulously cleaned the conch and extracted the sample, how he had used micro-drilling to obtain organic inclusions from the gem, and how he had isolated the leather remnants from the mace.

To further reassure Arvind, Vikas shared the detailed reports and photographs of each step of the analysis. He sent over the documented procedures and the data charts, highlighting the consistency and reliability of the results. "I know this is hard to accept, but the evidence is clear. These items are not as old as we thought. It's possible that they were crafted to appear ancient, but the science doesn't lie."

Arvind was silent for a moment as he reviewed the evidence Vikas had sent. Despite his initial resistance, the thorough explanation and the incontrovertible data began to sink in. "I see," he finally said, his voice tinged with resignation. "It's just... I had such high hopes for these artifacts."

"I understand, Arvind," Vikas replied sympathetically. "It's disappointing for both of us. But it's better to know the truth. We can move forward from here and focus on finding genuine artifacts."

Though still processing the shock, Arvind thanked Vikas for his diligence and honesty. They agreed to discuss their next steps in person, acknowledging that while this setback was significant, their dedication to their work and the search for historical truth remained unwavering.

Arvind was devastated by the revelation that the three artifacts were fake. In his deep disappointment, he knew he had to share this disheartening news with the rest of the group. He quickly arranged a conference call, not even bothering to use his secret secondary phone, which he usually reserved for sensitive communications. The urgency of the situation and the weight of the bad news overshadowed his usual caution.

As the members joined the call, curiosity and anticipation filled the virtual room. It had been over six weeks since their last meeting in Dwarka, and everyone was eager for an update. Arvind's voice, however, immediately set a somber tone. "Thank you all for joining on such short notice," he began, his voice heavy with dejection, sorrow, and hopelessness. "I have some bad news to share. The artifacts... the conch, the gem, and the mace... they are all fake."

A shocked silence followed his words. The group members, who had placed so much hope and anticipation in these items, were stunned. Rakesh, who had been clinging to a faint hope that these artifacts might provide some breakthrough for his son's treatment, was the first to break down. "No, this can't be true," he sobbed. "We were so sure... how could this happen?" His tears flowed freely as the reality of the situation sank in.

Gautam, who had struggled throughout his life and had seen these artifacts as a potential turning point, felt his heart shatter at the news. "This was supposed to be our chance, Arvind," he said, his voice cracking. "I thought... I thought this would finally change things for us." The hopelessness in his voice mirrored the despair that Arvind himself felt.

Other members of the group, equally devastated, became silent. The weight of the collective disappointment was palpable. One by one, they began to drop off the call, unable to find words to express their feelings or to offer comfort to one another. The silence that followed was heavy with unspoken grief and lost hope.

Arvind, left alone on the call, felt a profound sense of failure. He had hoped to bring good news, to validate their efforts and sacrifices. Instead, he had to deliver a crushing blow. He sat in silence, listening to the empty line, reflecting on the journey that had led them to this point.

The Chiranjeevis finally arrived back at Gangkhar Puensum, Bhutan, their spirits high with the thrill of success. The majestic mountain stood before them, cloaked in an ethereal veil of mist. Its snow-capped peaks glistened under the soft morning sun, casting long shadows across the serene landscape. The air was crisp and carried the faint scent of pine and earth, a reminder of the untouched purity of this remote sanctuary.

The path they had taken was winding and narrow, bordered by vibrant rhododendron forests that whispered tales of ancient legends. Along the trail, prayer flags fluttered gently in the breeze, their colors vivid against the stark whiteness of the snow. These flags, strung by pilgrims and adventurers alike, symbolized peace, compassion, and wisdom—qualities that the Chiranjeevis had embodied throughout their quest.

The Chiranjeevis slowly trod a path that had never been taken by any living being in the area, a hidden trail intricately camouflaged by towering trees. These ancient sentinels seemed to guard the way, their dense foliage creating a canopy that filtered the sunlight into delicate, dancing patterns on the forest floor. Each step they took was accompanied by the soft rustle of leaves and the distant calls of unseen birds, adding to the mystical atmosphere.

As they ventured deeper, the forest thickened, its age-old trees standing like silent witnesses to their journey. The air grew cooler and fresher, carrying the faint, earthy scent of moss and damp wood. After what felt like hours, they emerged into a secluded clearing, a sanctuary untouched by time. Tall, ageless trees encircled the space, their branches stretching skyward in a protective embrace.

In the heart of this natural haven, a small stream meandered gracefully near rocky banks adorned with small, beautiful white pebbles. The water, clear as crystal, gurgled softly as it flowed, its gentle sound creating a serene melody that filled the air. Sunlight peeked through the canopy, casting a golden glow on the stream and illuminating the pebbles, which sparkled like scattered gems. The Chiranjeevis felt a profound sense of peace wash over them as they stood in this untouched paradise, a testament to nature's enduring beauty and the secrets it held within its depths.

During their brief sojourn in the modern world with mortal identities, they forged many connections that they ultimately had to abandon. Bali, who lived as a coconut farmer in Kerala, was like a divine blessing to an elderly couple who missed Ramesh, as they had come to know him, like a son. Raghavan learned from his neighbor, a shopkeeper, about a creditor seeking repayment, but Hanuman never returned to the beach market, leaving Raghavan and the shopkeeper both curious and expectant.

Parshuram had become an integral member of the dance community in Parlakhemundi. In the few days he spent there, he built strong, affectionate bonds with the children who learned from and admired him. His sudden disappearance left the elderly members and students of the community feeling a profound sense of loss. Parshuram's Ranapa sticks, symbols of inspiration to many, remained as a reminder of his influence.

The corner of the ghat where Vyasa used to sit and wait for customers was soon taken over by another priest, who began performing rituals by the banks of the Ganga, filling the void left by Vyasa.

In Sri Lanka, Vibhishana made both great friends and envious rivals during his time as a cook. His Kurakkan Puttu was dearly missed by the eatery's customers. The owner searched for Vibhishana for weeks, but to no avail, and eventually hired a new cook, though he wished daily for the return of his beloved chef.

Ashwatthama had kept his promise and built a house for the old fisherman, who would never forget his kindness and remained grateful forever. The gesture deeply touched the fisherman, securing Ashwatthama's place in his heart.

Chiranjeevis settled on several rock platforms after a long journey. Once they reached their so-called home, they reverted to their original avatars. Their surroundings were serene, the ancient rocks providing a stable foundation for their rest. The air was filled with a sense of timelessness, reflecting their eternal nature. Upon returning to their true forms, they felt a renewed sense of purpose.

Bali proposed a plan to his fellow immortals. He suggested that they gather all the sacred elements required to prepare the elixir of immortality and consume it themselves. His reasoning was straightforward yet profound: since they were already blessed with immortality, drinking the elixir would prevent it from ever falling into the wrong hands. The elixir, once consumed, would be out of reach of mortals and those with malevolent intentions who might misuse its power. The immortals considered Bali's proposal carefully. They understood the gravity of the situation; the elixir held immense power and, in the wrong hands, could disrupt the balance of the universe. Bali's suggestion was driven by a desire to protect this balance.

Vyasa, the revered sage, disclosed a crucial aspect of the curse that Lord Vishnu had placed upon the sacred items. According to Vyasa, the elixir of immortality could only be created by mortals or beings who were not immortal. This revelation shocked the immortals, as it meant they were powerless to assemble the elixir themselves. Immortals could neither destroy the sacred items nor combine them to form the coveted elixir.

Understanding this profound limitation, the immortals realized why they were deemed the best guardians of the sacred items. Since they could not create the elixir, they were the ideal protectors, ensuring that the items remained safe and out of the reach of those who might misuse them. Vyasa's revelation highlighted the wisdom in Lord Vishnu's curse; it was a safeguard to maintain the balance and order of the universe.

The immortals accepted this responsibility with renewed determination. They fortified their resolve to guard the sacred items, knowing their immortality made them uniquely suited for this eternal task. Their inability to manipulate the sacred items was a testament to the divine foresight that had entrusted them with this duty. Thus, the sacred items remained protected, and their secrets and powers were kept safe from any mortal ambitions.

Arvind looked at the notebook his grandfather had given him. In it, he had meticulously noted all the information he had gathered over the last two decades, following the ancient ritual his ancestors had practiced. As he gazed at the notebook, a sense of contemplation washed over him. He pondered the right moment to pass this legacy to the next generation. The memories of hardship, failures, and hopelessness he had endured on this quest came flooding back, raising doubts in his mind about whether he truly wanted to pass this burden to his son.

For over twenty years, Arvind had pursued this ritual with unwavering dedication. He had faced countless obstacles, many of which had tested his resolve to the breaking point. There were nights when he felt utterly defeated, questioning the purpose of his efforts. The notebook held stories of both triumphs and setbacks, a testament to his relentless pursuit. Yet, as he reflected on his journey, he couldn't ignore the emotional toll it had taken on him.

Arvind thought of his son, wondering if he wanted him to experience the same struggles. The quest had shaped him, molded him into who he was, but at what cost? The decision weighed heavily on his heart. Did he want to bestow this legacy, fraught with challenges and uncertainties, upon the next generation? As he closed the notebook, a deep sigh escaped his lips. The answer eluded him, leaving him in a state of introspection, caught between the duty to honor his ancestors and the desire to protect his son's future.

As Arvind casually flipped through the pages of the notebook, his eyes fell upon a page that stood out. A large circle was drawn on it, with the word "Jeevan" inscribed boldly in the center. A smile spread across Arvind's face as he immediately related it to the circle of life. It struck him deeply, for he realized he was once again standing at the same crossroads where he had begun many years ago.

The memories of his early days on this journey came rushing back. He had been full of hope and ambition, ready to take on the challenges that lay ahead. The circle symbolized continuity and the cyclical nature of existence, something he had come to understand profoundly over the years. It reminded him of the endless cycle of beginnings and endings, triumphs and failures, hopes and despair.

As he traced the outline of the circle with his finger, he felt a sense of completion, despite the unresolved questions that still lingered in his mind. He had come full circle, experiencing the highs and lows that life had to offer. The word "Jeevan" encapsulated his entire journey, a journey that had brought him back to his roots, his starting point. In that moment, Arvind felt a connection to the past and an understanding of the present, realizing that life, in all its complexity, always brings one back to where it all began.

Despite his devastation, he knew that this was a pivotal moment. They had to regroup, reassess, and find a way to move forward. He resolved to meet with the group in person as soon as possible. They needed to support each other and figure out their next steps. The fake artifacts were a significant setback, but Arvind believed that their shared determination and resilience would ultimately guide them through this dark moment. Although the road ahead seemed bleak, he knew they couldn't give up. They had come too far and endured too much to let this defeat them.

www.ingramcontent.com/pod-product-compliance
Lightning Source LLC
Chambersburg PA
CBHW060546160726
47991CB00001B/458